Robert Lord Lytton

Fables in Song

Vol. I.

Robert Lord Lytton

Fables in Song
Vol. I.

ISBN/EAN: 9783337100865

Printed in Europe, USA, Canada, Australia, Japan

Cover: Foto ©Andreas Hilbeck / pixelio.de

More available books at **www.hansebooks.com**

FABLES IN SONG

FABLES IN SONG

BY

ROBERT LORD LYTTON

AUTHOR OF 'POEMS BY OWEN MEREDITH'

VOL. I.

WILLIAM BLACKWOOD AND SONS
EDINBURGH AND LONDON
MDCCCLXXIV

CONTENTS OF THE FIRST VOLUME.

INTRODUCTORY.

1.

Had I miss'd my way? It would seem so. Still,
Scarce past is an hour of the matin prime
Since safe I was sitting in front of the mill ;
Where my first walk ever, this pure May time,
Under the beeches, and round by the rill,
'Twixt brawling ripple, and rustling bough,
Hath its wonted end, by the brook ; that, now
When the sweet birds sing together,
Carolling clear in the cool, comes down
From the breezy hills, and the sunburnt heather ;
Guided about to his goal unknown
By a glimmer of primrose buds new blown,
And their breath on the balmy weather.

2.

Well, there by the mill, as I say,
Where, between them, the brook and the bough
For my sake make a musical bower,
Safe I sat in the morn of the day ;
And since there I was sitting, I vow
That the day is scarce older an hour.
But now ?
Where am I ? who ought to know
Every inch of this leafy land.
Yet here, but a step at the most, or two,
From the door of the well-known mill
(Which all the while must be near at hand,
For the sound of it follows me still)
I am lost in a forest whose glades expand
O'er me, before me, immense and dense ;
Where shadow and sighing sound profound
Pour into my spirit a sense intense
Of dimness and distance ; and, turning around
And around myself, I no further have got
Than the wheel of that mill, which, the more to
        confound
My confusion, I hear, tho' I see it not.

3.

I did well to be on my guard!
Tho' my caution avail'd not much.
One step more over the sward
Which had seem'd so safe and hard,
And the grass, or whatever I took for such,
Giving suddenly way at my foot's first touch,
Down with it, down, I fell
Into the depths of a dell
Sunless and silent and deep
As the dim caverns of sleep.

4.

There, thro' the gloom in distress
Gazing around, I could see
That some four-footed stray-away less
Keen of eye, or of footstep steady
Than I myself, had been caught already
By the snare which had thus caught me.
In the hug of those horrible rocks,
Unacquainted companions we,
Like two vagabonds set in the stocks.
But what could the creature be?
A fox? Was it, truly, a fox?
Ha! how got the rascal here?

No matter! he gets not out.
'Tis the end of his bad career.

5.

Yet *is* it a fox ?   I doubt,
Now the gleam of his eyes grow clear
Thro' the dim light round about.
From the look in those wistful eyes
Who could possibly recognise
The rogue whose rascalities bold,
By farmwife and fabulist told,
Have so ruin'd his reputation ?
What a sadness of resignation !

6.

And he seem'd to me wondrous old.

7.

I thought, as he eyed me so,
He was asking pity from man:
Tho' needs must the rascal know
Men have put him under their ban.
My soul was grieved, I confess,
At the sight of the brute's distress,
And I mutter'd, " Poor Reynard ! I see

Thou art lean and grey as a ghost,
And the few teeth, age at the most
Hath spared thee, are worn to a stump.
If I can, I will set thee free.
For the miller's pullets, tho' plump,
Have nothing to fear from thee.
And 'tis never too late to mend.
Trust me ! I speak as a friend."

8.

He seem'd to understand ;
Crept closer, and lick'd my hand.
" There, there ! we are friends.   But how
To get out of this horrible hole ?
Ha ! some issue, seems yonder : and now
Up I climb by the oak-tree bole.
Leap on my shoulder.   Hold fast.
Well clamber'd ! welcome the goal !
Thou art safe on thy road at last.
And I heartily wish I could say
As much for myself: but, aghast,
I perceive I have miss'd my way."

9.

Yet the creature will not go.
He lingers : and still he eyes me

With those wonderful eyes, as tho'
(Do they bless, beseech, or advise me?)
There were something, still, he wanted.
" What is it ?   Speak, then, speak !
Nothing can now surprise me ;
Except that the spell should break.
For I think I am here in a forest enchanted,
And, if I can grant it, thy prayer is granted."

10.

" Thou hast help'd me.   I thank thee, man."
" What magic my fancy mocks ? "
" And will help thee, too, if I can."
" What art thou ? "   Sadly the fox
Said, " I am the ancient Fox of Fable.
Few are the men I have met with, able
To understand me ; and still more few
The men that listen to those who do."

11.

" What ! " I exclaim'd, " thou hast known, then,
        thou,
That spiteful hunchback, old Æsop ? "—" I know
That Æsop," he answer'd in scorn,
" Hath no hump on his honest back ;

And, never having been born,
He never hath died." " Alack !
Thou art, indeed, I perceive,
The Fox of Fable !   Pray,
What next wilt thou have me believe ? "

12.

" That Æsop is living today."
" Where, prithee ? "

13.

" In me : in thee :
For he lives in each living creature
(Man, beast, bird, blossom, and tree),
And his life is the love of nature.
The complaint, that was half a caress,
Men have turn'd into bitterness :
The counsel, cordial and bland,
To a churlish reprimand :
Justice, robed in her ruth,
To Resentment eager to smite :
And Sagacity, Humour, and Truth,
Into Sarcasm, Satire, and Spite.
Thus, alas ! when, to banish the true,
A false Æsop you form'd, of your own,

We, the children of Æsop, withdrew.
For we found that to leave you alone
Was then all you had left to us.   Few
Are the men with whom now we are able
To converse, as our wont was of old :
And, afar in the Forest of Fable,
With, between us, a world sad and cold,
Safe we dwell, out of your view.
But, O man, thou hast open'd thy heart
Unto mine, and thus broken the spell :
So my thanks prithee take, ere we part,
In the language of Fable.   Farewell ! "

14.

" Stay ! " I cried, " one last word, I implore !
Must that word be farewell, fellow-creature ?
May we meet, then, no more, no more,
In the motherly arms of Nature ?
Ah, those friendly voices of yore !
Could I hear them, I fain would record
All they said to me; writing it down
Simply, honestly, true to a word."

15.

" My part I have done.   Do thine own,"
Said the Fox (as we turn'd, and stood

Where, pleasantly welcoming me,
Peep'd the mill, once more, thro' the wood)
" Love us, and—we shall see."

16.

" Love you ? " I cried ; " but what use in that,
If I never may meet you again ?
Never mingle among you in brotherly chat !
Must I love, and yet seek you in vain ? "
The Fox hesitated, then sigh'd,
" Ah, friend, have you ever yet tried ?
They fail not to find us, who seek,
Though disguised do we go amongst men.
Approach, I say, question, and speak
Heart to heart with all creatures : and then,
 . . . Well, hast thou not spoken to me
From thy heart? and mine own, was it dumb?"

17.

" Then," I said, " whatsoever they be
That I meet, as the chance may come,
If I speak to, and question, them all—
Bees that hover, and blossoms that hum ;
The beast of the field or the stall ;
The trees, leaves, rushes, and grasses ;

The rivulet, running away;
The bird of the air, as it passes ;
Or the mountains, that motionless stay ;
And yet whose irremovable masses
Keep changing, as dreams do, all day ;
Will they answer me ?   Tell me, O tell !
For, look you, I love them well."

18.

The Fox, as he turn'd aside,
Gave me a friendly glance ;
And, fading into the forest, replied
With encouraging voice, " Perchance.
Try ! "   And so . . .   Well, I have tried.

FABLES IN SONG.

I.

THE THISTLE.

MOTTO.

(*A Flower's Ballad.*)

IT was a thorn,
And it stood forlorn
In the burning sunrise land:

A blighted thorn,
And at eve and morn
Thus it sigh'd to the desert sand —

" Every flower,
By it's beauty's power,
With a crown of glory is crown'd.

" No crown have I,
For a crown I sigh,
For a crown that I have not found.

" A crown ! a crown !
A crown of mine own,
To wind in a maiden's hair!"

Sad thorn, why grieve ?
Thou a crown shalt weave,
But not for a maiden to wear.

That crown shall shine
When all crowns save thine,
With the glory they gave, are gone :

For, thorn, my thorn,
Thy crown shall be worn
By the King of Sorrows alone.

PRELUDE.

The green grass-blades aquiver
    With joy at the dawn of day
(For the most inquisitive ever
    Of the flowers of the field are they)
Lisp'd it low to their lazy
    Neighbours that flat on the ground,
Dandelion and daisy,
    Lay still in a slumber sound :
But soon, as a ripple of shadow
    Runs over the whisperous wheat,
The rumour ran over the meadow
    With its numberless fluttering feet :

It was told by the water-cresses
　To the brooklet that, in and out
Of his garrulous green recesses,
　For gossip was gadding about :
And the brooklet, full of the matter,
　Spread it abroad with pride ;
But he stopp'd to gossip and chatter,
　And turn'd so often aside,
That his news got there before him
　Ere his journey down was done ;
And young leaves in the vale laugh'd o'er him
　" We know it !　THE SNOW IS GONE ! "
The snow is gone ! but ye only
Know how good doth that good news sound,
　Whose hearts, long buried and lonely,
　Have been waiting, winter-bound,
For the voice of the wakening angel
　To utter the welcome evangel,
　" The snow is gone : reärise,
　　And blossom as heretofore,
　Hopes, imaginings, memories,
　　And joys of the days of yore !"

What are the tree-tops saying, swaying
　This way all together ?
" The winter is past ! the south wind at last
　Is come, and the sunny weather !"
The trees ! there is no mistaking them,
For the trees, they never mistake :

And you may tell, by the way of the stem,
  What the way is, the wind doth take.
So, if the tree-tops nod this way,
  It is the south wind that is come ;
And, if to the other side nod they,
  Go, clothe ye warm, or bide at home !
The flowers all know what the tree-tops say ;
  They are no more deaf than the trees are dumb.
And they do not wait to hear it twice said
  If the news be good ; but, discreet and gay,
The awaked buds dance from their downy bed,
With pursed-up mouth, and with peeping head,
  By many a dim green winding way.

  'Tis the white anemone, fashion'd so
  Like to the stars of the winter snow,
  First thinks, " If I come too soon, no doubt
I shall seem but the snow that hath staid too long,
  So 'tis I that will be Spring's unguess'd scout."
  And wide she wanders the woods among.
  Then, from out of the mossiest hiding-places,
    Smile meek moonlight-colour'd faces
      Of pale primroses puritan,
    In maiden sisterhoods demure ;
    Each virgin flowret faint and wan
  With the bliss of her own sweet breath so pure.
  And the borage, blue-eyed, with a thrill of pride,
    (For warm is her welcome on every side)
  From Elfland coming to claim her place,
    Gay garments of verdant velvet takes

All creased from the delicate travelling case
   Which a warm breeze breaks. The daisy awakes
And opens her wondering eyes, yet red
   About the rims with a too long sleep ;
Whilst, bold from his ambush, with helm on head
   And lance in rest, doth the bulrush leap.

The violets meet, and disport themselves,
   Under the trees, by tens and twelves.
The timorous cowslips, one by one,
   Trembling, chilly, atiptoe stand
On little hillocks and knolls alone ;
   Watchful pickets, that wave a hand
For signal sure that the snow is gone,
     Then around them call their comrades all
     In a multitudinous, mirthful band ;
Till the field is so fill'd with grass and flowers
   That wherever, with flashing footsteps, fall
The sweet, fleet, silvery April showers,
   They never can touch the earth, which is
     Cover'd all over with crocuses,
And the clustering gleam of the buttercup,
And the blithe grass blades that stand straight up
And make themselves small, to leave room for all
     The nameless blossoms that nestle between
     Their sheltering stems in the herbage green ;
     Sharp little soldiers, trusty and true,
       Side by side in good order due ;
     Arms straight down, and heads forward set,
       And saucily-pointed bayonet.

Up the hillocks, and down again,
The green grass marches into the plain,
If only a light wind over the land
Whisper the welcome word of command.

PART I.

'Twas long after the grass and the flowers, one day,
That there came straggling along the way
A little traveller, somewhat late.
Tired he was ; and down he sat
In the ditch by the road, where he tried to nestle
Out of the dust and the noontide heat.
Poor little vagabond wayside Thistle !
In the ditch was his only safe retreat.
Flung out of the field as soon as found there,
And banisht the garden, where should he stay ?
Wherever he roam'd, still Fortune frown'd there,
And, wherever he settled, spurn'd him away.

From place to place, had he wander'd long
The weary high road, parcht with thirst.
Now here, in the ditch, for awhile among
The brambles hidden, he crouch'd ; and first
Wistfully eyed, on the other side,
A fresh green meadow with flowrets pied ;
And then, with a pang, as he peep'd and pried,
" Oh, to rest there !" he thought, and sigh'd.

" Oh, to rest there, it is all so fair !
Yonder wanders a brooklet, sure ?
No ! it is only the mill-sluice small.
But he looks like a brook, so bright and pure,
    And his banks are broider'd with violets all.
What a hurry he seems to be in ! Ah, why
    Doth he hasten so fast ? If I were he,
There would I linger, and rest, and try
To be left in peace. Take heed ! (ah me,
    He doth not hear me—how weary I am !)
Take heed, for the sake of thine old mill-dam,
    Thou little impetuous fool ! I pass'd
Over the bridge, as I came by the road ;
    And under the bridge I saw rolling fast
A full-grown river, so deep and broad !
If you go on running like that—nor look
    Where you are running—you foolish brook,
I predict you will fall into trouble at last,
    And the great big river will eat you up.
That is all you will get by your heedless haste.
    Oh, if I were you, it is there I'd stop,
There where you are, with the flowers and grass.
For I know what it is to wander, alas !
    It is only to fall from bad to worse,
    And find no rest in the universe.

" Soft !—I have half a mind to try—
    Could one slip in yonder quietly,
Where the rippled damp of the deep grass spares
    Cool rest to each roving butterfly,

How pleasant 'twould be ! There is nobody by,
  And perhaps there is nobody owns or cares
To look after yon meadow. It seems so still,
Silent, and safe—shall I venture ?—I will !
  From the ditch it is but a step or two.
And, maybe, the owner is dead, and the heirs
  Away in the town, and will never know."

PART II.

Then the little Thistle atiptoe stood,
  All in a tremble, sharp yet shy.
The vagabond's conscience was not good.
  He had been so often a trespasser sly,
He had been so often caught by the law,
  He had been so often beaten before :
He was still so small : if a spade he saw,
  He mutter'd a *Paternoster* o'er,
And cower'd. So, cautiously thrusting out
Here a timorous leaf, there a tiny sprout,
And then dropping a seed, and so waiting anon
For a chance lift got from the wind—still on,
With a hope that the sun and the breeze migh
    please
To be helpful and kind—by degrees he frees
And feels his way with a fluttering heart.
  In the ditch there were heaps of stones to pass.
They scratch'd him, and tore him, and made him
    smart,

And ruin'd his leaves.   But those leaves, alas,
 Already so tatter'd and shatter'd were,
That to keep them longer was worth no care ;
And at last he was safe in the meadow ; and there
 " Ah, ha !" sigh'd the Thistle ; " so far, so well !
If I can but stay where I am, I shall fare
Blithe as the bee in the blossom's bell.
How green it is here, and how fresh, and fair !
 And, oh, what a pleasure henceforth to dwell
In this blest abode ! to have done with the road,
 And got rid of the ditch !   Ah, who can tell
 The rapture of rest to the wanderer's breast ? "

 Down out of heaven a dewdrop fell
On the head of the Thistle : and he fell asleep
In the lap of the twilight soft and deep.

PART III.

 At sunrise he woke : and he still was there,
 In the bright grass, breathing the balmy air.
He stretch'd his limbs, and he shook off the dust,
 And he wash'd himself in the morning dew ;
And, opening his pedlar's pack, out-thrust
 A spruce little pair of leaflets new;
And made for himself a fine white ruff,
 About his neck to wear ;
And pruned and polish'd his prickles tough ;
 And put on a holiday air.

And "If only nobody finds me out!"
He laugh'd, as he loll'd among
The grass, delighted, and look'd about,
And humm'd a homely song;
Which he loved because, like himself, 'twas known
As a wanderer here and there,

" A crown ! a crown !
A crown of mine own,
To wind in a maiden's hair ! "

But . . . a sweep of the scythe, and a stamp of the foot,
And "Vile weed! is there no getting rid of thee
ever?"
And what little was spared by the scythe, the boot,
With its hobnails, hasten'd to crush and shiver.

PART IV.

'Twas the Farmer, who just then happen'd to pass.
He had gone to the field to cut some grass
For his beast that morn; and no sooner saw
The trespasser there *in flagrante delicto,*
Than, scythe in hand, he enforced the law
On the luckless offender, *vi et ictu.*

All mangled and bruised, the poor little Thistle
With his desperate roots to the soil clung fast.
The Farmer away, with a careless whistle,
Homeward over the meadow pass'd.

The Thistle breathed freër, and shook his gasht head.
"All's well, if it be no worse!" he said.
" My crown is gone, but 'twill grow again.
There is many another (*I feel it*) in me.
And one must not make too much of the pain.
Only, you good saints, let me not be
Forced, for my sins, to return to the road !
Only not that ! If I can but contrive
To rest here, somehow or other !   I see
One may lose his head in this brave abode.
But I'm on my guard, and I'll struggle and strive,
As long as I live, to keep alive."
Then his roots he burrow'd more deep and broad.

But every day 'twas the self-same thing!
Tho' he made himself little, and hid his head,
Trying, with all his might, to cling
Close to the soil, and appear to be dead.
For his spacious leaves, that were carved and curl'd
For Corinthian columns in temples fair,
He could not check them when these unfurl d
Their flourishing architecture there,
And, all about him their beauty spreading,
Layer on layer uprose from below ;
And the hardy young head, in despite of beheading,
Sprang up again—for the scythe to mow !
Round and about him, each blossom was blowing.
No chance of blowing had *he* found ever :
Who no sooner was seen than the sharp steel mowing,
Or the harsh foot crushing him, stopp'd the endeavour.

And "Oh, blessèd," he sigh'd, "is the blossom that
    blows !
    Colours I know of, no eyes yet see.
But I dare not show them ; and nobody knows,
    Nobody guesses, what's hidden in me !
    In all the world but one creature, alas,
For love's sake seeks me ; and *he* is an ass."

PART V.

So went the Spring : and so came and went
    The Summer. The aftermath was mown :
And there where, erewhile, in one element
    Of colour and odour together blent,
By the balmy breath of the light wind blown,
The flowing grass and the bending blooms
    (A rapturous river of gleams and glooms !)
Had rippled and roll'd, lay clods of mould
    Black and bald ; and between them grew
Coarse aftergrowths, grey, bristly, and cold ;
    And the beast of the field had the residue.
    The primrose, cowslip, and violet,
With their glow-worm glitter were gone ; and the white
    Anemone's constellations, set,
    Had left the earth dark as a starless night,
Where the grass fell off from the woodland wet.
    The blue-eyed borage was blinded quite.
    But, outliving his betters one by one,
    In the flowerless field, with no thought of flight,

The brave little Thistle remain'd—alone !
And, since skies were cold, and suns were dim,
No one noticed, and no one praised,
But also no one *maltreated*, him.
And the pensive beasts of the field, that grazed
The twice-cropt grass, where their wandering whim
Led them, lazy, from spot to spot,
Shunn'd the Thistle and harm'd him not.

PART VI.

Then the Thistle, at last, could enlarge his store
Of the few joys fate had vouchsafed him sparely.
Baffled a hundred times, and more,
Bruised, and torn, and surviving barely,
Still he *survived :* and for him, him only,
Green leaves gladden'd the leafless cold
Where, Summer's orphan, he linger'd lonely
Over her grave in the frozen mould.
For, as days, long dead, by a bard born after
Are invoked, and revive in a form more fair,
All the bliss that was beauty, the life that was laughter,
Ere the frolic fields were bereft and bare,
The lone Thistle renew'd and transform'd to his own ;
As flower by flower—from the fervid rose,
Whose beauty so well to herself is known,
That she blushes proud of the truth she knows,
To the violet, Modesty's vanquisht child,
Hiding her head in the sylvan places

Where her wandering wooer, the March gust wild,
    Hath left her faint from his harsh embraces,
        All of them—all, in a dream divine
To the heart of the Thistle sweet secrets told
        Of blushes that burn, and of brows that shine,
            With passion of purple and glory of gold.
So all flowers of the field were alive in one :
        And the glow of his sheen, and the gloss of his down,
Were as jewels dead queens have confided alone
    To the craftsman who fashions them all to a crown.

For each hope in the heart of the poor plant hidden
    Each vision of bliss and of beauty, nurst,
With a passion by Prejudice check'd and chidden,
    For a life by the fiat of Fortune curst,
Rushing forthwith into rich reality,
        Fill'd the cup of a quenchless thirst
Till it flow'd with exuberant prodigality,
        And his long-pent life into blossom burst.
        A single blossom : but statelier far,
        And fairer, than many a million are.
A splendid disc, full and flashing with wonder !
        As the sea-rose swims on the water, so
That effulgent star on the bleak earth under
        Lay spread out in a luminous glow.
And " At last I can blossom ! blossom ! blossom ! "
    The Thistle laugh'd, greeting the earth and heaven,
And he blossom'd his whole heart out of his bosom.

    And all was forgotten, save all that was given.

II.

POSSESSION.

A Poet loved a Star,
And to it whisper'd nightly,
" Being so fair, why art thou, love, so far?
Or why so coldly shine, who shinest so brightly ?
 O Beauty, woo'd and unpossest,
 O might I to this beating breast
 But clasp thee once, and then die, blest ! "

That Star her Poet's love,
So wildly warm, made human.
And, leaving for his sake her heaven above,
His Star stoop'd earthward, and became a Woman.
 " Thou who hast woo'd and hast possest,
 My lover, answer, which was best,
 The Star's beam, or the Woman's breast ? "

" I miss from heaven," the man replied,
 " A light that drew my spirit to it."
And to the man the woman sigh'd,
 " I miss from earth a poet."

III.

WHO'S IN THE RIGHT?

PRELUDE.

A BATTERY, posted in haste, at last,
On the brow of a hill in the foeman's flank,
Had decided the fate of the day.   Fast, fast,
In many a broken and billowy rank
The bewilder'd rear of his battle fled.
But, rapid behind, like a rushing wind
That rattles with hail, to the lowland red
Down from the ridge of the smoky hill,
The cavalry clash'd in a clattering shower ;
Crushing the harvest, and chasing still
All that was left of a nation's power.

And wide it swept over the wasted plain,
That rapture of ruin, red in the glare
Of burning barns ; and the bolted rain
Sang thro' the blacken'd and sulphurous air,
As in storm it stream'd and subsided again ;

Till all was still save the far-off blare
Of a ghostly bugle, echoing chill ;
Whose echoes, heard by the yet unslain
O'er leagues of litter, from hill to hill
Proclaim'd that the hurly-burly was done :
A kingdom lost and a kingdom won !

PART I.

1.

In that hollow battery's earthen mound,
Gaily gather'd the guns around,
The officers, free at the fall of the day,
Were discussing with whom the achievement lay
Of so great a success.　And said one of them, " Friends,
" Was there ever a captain so skill'd in war
As our gallant Prince ?　Bright Victory wends
With him, wherever his flag flies, far
From city to city ; and lucky are we
Whose fortunes follow the guiding star
Of a hero, whose genius, all agree,
Is as great as his glorious actions are."
Another, in answer, his shoulders shrugg'd,
And " Ay," as his shaggy beard he tugg'd,
" So is every conqueror styled," quoth he,
" Though owed to others his conquests be.
But the few to whom war's art is known
Know 'tis the General Staff alone

That organises and orders all ;
To each arm of the service assigns that place
Where best the effect of its force may fall,
And the plan of the whole campaign doth trace."
" 'May be," said a third, " that by these and those,
In a general way, is good service done.
No fruit can ripen, of course one knows,
Without the assistance of soil and sun.
But the question is—when your fruit is ripe,
How to pluck it." (And here, his pipe
He lit, as he added) " That, you see,
" Can only be done by the Cavalry."
" You forget," said a fourth, an Engineer,
" The man who posted this battery here.
The foe had out-number'd us, ten to one,
And would, but for him, have o'erwhelm'd us too."
" Posted the battery ? Easily done !"
A sergeant mutter'd.   " Forget not, you,
" Which of us was it, that pointed the gun."

2.

'Neath the battery wall where these conversed,
A wounded gunner unheeded lay ;
By a random shell, that had near him burst,
His feet were shatter'd and shorn away.
His lips were baked by a burning thirst,
On his limbs did the icy ague prey :

The yet smouldering brand in his frozen hand
He grasp'd ; and follow'd, with eyes aflame,
The far-off blaze, that greeted his gaze
With the deadly effect of his life's last aim.
Not a word had he heard
Of the talk around him.
He died.   And, with pride
In death dealt, death crown'd him.
Pain's parcht furrows placidly glided
Out of his weather-beaten face ;
But a silent smile of triumph slided,
Under death's hovering hand, in their place ;
And death, for a sign, congeal'd it there,
Stern, and fair.

3.

Now, of all the glory that gilt that day
Not a gleam yet glows in these after ages.
All that glitter'd hath faded away ;
All, save the name of the Prince ; in her pages
By History written, though seldom read.
All else is dead.

PART II.

1.

Clio, with clarion, palm, and book,
Pass on !   Not thine are we.

Thy plainer sister's shepherd crook
We follow ; seeking flowers forsook,
That breathe about the rural brook,
And win the wandering bee.

What History oft, in stately pride,
With haughty gesture spurns aside,
Wild Fable from the wayside field
Picks up, and lays to heart.
And truths, by her to us reveal'd,
Do we to you impart:

2.

How that bronze tube, round which erewhile
This discussion was carried so high,
Mock'd, as it listen'd, and said with a smile,
" Men boast, but the victor am I ! "
" Thou?" growl'd the Cannon Ball—" thou ! is it thou
Who didst level yon walls with the plain,
Mowing down men, as the harvesters mow
Hollow paths thro' the thick of the grain ?
Braggart ! 'tis I who alone can do this.
'Tis the brush of my brazen orb bursts wide
War's mason'd masses !"—Whereto, with a hiss,
" Silence, blockhead !" the Powder replied.
" On the arsenal floor had'st thou rested still,
Were it not for me, who thy wings provide.
And thou art but the deed: it is I am the will."
But, as thus he mutter'd, with surly pride,

" Vagabond !" scornfully splutter'd the Match,
" Boast not thou in thy master's presence !
Ball, Cannon, and Powder,—inert batch
Of base stuff, stirr'd by my quickening essence,—
The Fire am I, and my slaves are ye.
He, whose vitals a vulture tore,
Well was he 'ware of the worth of me,
When from heaven he stole, in the days of yore,
The spark that in my Promethean wand
Yet glows with the heat of a god's invention."

3.

" Attention ! "
An officer cried, in command.

4.

For faint, and afar, with a dying spasm,
The bruised-out battle was breathing again.
And the gun was charged, from his gaping chasm,
To clear it away from the cumber'd plain
Where it crawl'd in pain.

5.

The gunner pointed the gun to the mark.
With an eager spark
The ardent match, death's nimble adept,
To the touch-hole leapt.

And . . . . went out in the dark.
Not a groan, not a flame, from the great gun came,
Not a belch of smoke : unejected slept
In his burthen'd gullet the sullen bullet :
The captains were cursing, the gunners were grumbling,
And, drop upon droplet, as down it came tumbling,
Merrily, mockingly laugh'd the light Shower :
" O fools ! lo, I sprinkle a silvery twinkle
Of beads from my bosom, and where is your power ?
Black dust of death, art thou melted quite
Into a harmless unsavoury sop ?
What of your lightnings ? where is their light ?
Quencht in a quagmire, slain by a slop !
Your valorous thunders, voices of might ?
Struck dumb by a dancing drop ! "

6.

The dying Fire heard this,
And with a hiss
Spat out the scorn of his indignant hate,
" Demon of Impotence !
Boast not that thou art great,
Upon the poor pretence
Of greatness hinder'd and defeated by thee. .
Force to annihilate
Force, hast thou : but the gods deny thee
Force to create."

7.

" Stay, not so fast ! "
Sighingly answer'd him the streaming Rain.
" Destroyer, what hast *thou* created ?   Cast
On thy brief work (death, devastation, pain)
One glare—thy last !
Show me thy greatness.   Is it yonder plain
Where thou hast pass'd,
Leaving behind thee hideous heaps of slain
And ruin vast ?
Lo, with my little drops, I bless again
And beautify the fields which thou didst blast !
Rend, wither, waste, and ruin, what thou wilt,
But call not Greatness what the gods call Guilt.
Blossoms and grass from blood in battle spilt,
And poppied corn, I bring.
'Mid mouldering Babels, to Oblivion built,
My violets spring.
Little by little, my small drops have strength
To deck with green delights the grateful earth :
Little by little, to large seas at length
Small springs give birth :
By little things the growing world grows great,
And of great doings rests but little done :
From little fibres in the loom of Fate
Time's robe is spun :
Small are the cymbals that, when clasht, proclaim
The march of Force : from shafts of tiny stature

Co-operant atoms build the crystal frame
Of mighty Nature.
By little ducts Thought's widening river runs
Thro' nerve and brain, yet fills the ages vast,
And even the secret of the central suns
Invades at last :
In little waves light leaps from star to star :
Small pencils paint the welkin's azure pall :
And small life's primal universes are,
Yet they are all."

IV.

PREMATURITY.

1.

If aught in nature be unnatural,
  It is the slaying by a springtide frost
Of Spring's own children : cheated blossoms all,
Betray'd i' the birth, and born for burial
  Of budding promise, scarce beloved ere lost !
Once, in the silence of a clear Spring night,
This still, cold-footed Frost, with footstep light
  Slid thro' the tepid season, like a ghost
    Wrapt in thin white.
Flitting, he smote the first-born of the year,
And, ere the break of day, their pretty buds were sere.

2.

But the blossoms that perish'd
  Were those alone
Which, in haste to be cherish'd,
  With loosen'd zone
Had too soon to the sun all their beauty shown.

Lightly-vested,
Amorous-breasted,
Blossom of almond, blossom of peach :
Impatient children, with hearts unsteady,
So young, and yet more precocious each
Than the leaves of the Summer, and blushing already!

3.

These perish'd, because too soon they lived ;
But the oak flower, prudent and proud, survived.
" If the sun would win me," she thought, " he must
    Wait for me, wooing me warmly the while ;
For a flower's a fool, if a flower would trust
    Her whole sweet being to one first smile."

V.

ANCIENTS AND MODERNS.

1.

I' THE city of the ruins of the world
A rumour flutter'd, on that breeze unfurl'd
Whose puff-cheek'd Æolus is Public Prate,
That some vine's owner, digging the estate
Of classic dirt which lodged his lucky vine,
Had stumbled on a statue, Greek, and fine.

2.

Priests, princes, populace—Rome's papal fold
Prolific—rams and lambs—the young, the old—
The learnèd and unlearnèd—all came flocking
(Some clad in scarlet hat and purple stocking ;
Some, with no stockings, and no hats at all ;
But each as blithe as for a festival)
To gaze, and praise, and bless the favour'd spot,
Whence Rome, renascent, such a prize had got
Back from the ruins of herself.   For there,
In radiant resurrection, fresh and fair

As when that statue first with classic grace
The clement Cæsar's palace deck'd, i' the place
Where sank the baths of Titus from the sun,
Apollo's patriot priest, Laöcoön,
Reveal'd to Roman crowds, now Christian grown,
That Pagan Anguish which, in Parian stone,
The Rhodian artist had express'd so well
That here for ever Pain hath Beauty's spell.

3.

Down in the wreck and rummage of the ground
Wherein this famous statue had been found,
A snake, emergent from his clayey chasm,
Had watch'd with wonder Rome's enthusiasm.
And, when the crowd was gone, the reptile gazed
Upon the statue which the crowd had praised.
Laöcoön, and his sons, this snake esteem'd
But secondary parts of what he deem'd
The sculptor's main design.   As what one sees
(When painted, haply, by the Veronese)
Most to admire in Cana's banquet board,
For nuptial feast with goodly goblets stored
And viands spread—is not the wine and meat,
But the brave guests who drink it and who eat;
So, what this reptile deem'd the chiefest part
Of the whole group, and of its artist's art
The choicest specimen, was—naturally—
Not the mere victims of the slaughterous sally

Made by its kind on the Laöcoöns,
(Not even the father, and much less the sons)
Who for those snakes were as a banquet spread,
But the snakes' selves, who on that banquet fed.

4.

And "Is that all?" the ambitious reptile cried,
"As much, and more can I!" Then, puft with pride,
About the statue of a wrestler old,
That stood thereby, his fluctuous rings he roll'd,
Regurgitating gulfy waves, that wound
In sliding sinuous ripple round and round ;
Knotted the athlete's knees in cumbrous coil,
Clove to his stretcht throat, and with slimy toil
Strove to crush flat the swoll'n and starting throng
Of bulky sinews that, like bulwarks strong,
Buttress'd the large limbs of the marble man.
Thrice round the raised right arm the reptile ran
His rolling orbs ; and, winding in and out,
With clasp convulsive girt the breast about.

5.

In vain ! For not one massive muscle shrank,
Bruised by the writhing worm's embrace ; nor sank
The raised right arm ; nor groan'd the granite breast.
And the mute mouth its marble smile compress'd,
Calm as before, 'twixt serious lips serene.
Naught marr'd that noble form's majestic mien,

And gesture stern.   The sole disfigurement
Was its aggressor's ; as, with strength nigh spent,
The serpent strain'd.   The sole contortion shown
Was all its reptile rival's ; not its own.

6.

When the great gods, grown jealous of great men,
Great vengeance take on human greatness ; when
One grandeur to another, grander still,
Succumbs ; when the Divinity, whose will
Goads man with agony, doth not disdain
To beautify the expression of man's pain ;
When he, who doth with equal power inspire
The harmonious strings of the delightful lyre
And the fell serpent fangs of Tenedos,
Is King Apollo ; then, with loss on loss,
Albeit the waves of blind Oblivion   .
Wash out wide empires as they wander on,
Tho' slowly over temple, tower, and town,
Grow green the grass of Lethe's drowsy down,
And the dull weed of dark Forgetfulness
Round spotless statues its accurst caress
Do creeping wind,—yet this the gods vouchsafe :
If from the deep men save one wandering waif
Of wrecks that once immortal shapes have borne,
Still of some grace divine not all forlorn
Men's lives are left.   One fragment, if no more,
Of those great forms great thoughts have fill'd of yore,
Suffices Beauty to reveal her will,
Marr'd, murder'd, buried, but triumphant still !

7.

Well-meaning, but unwise, contortionists
Of our well-meaning times, whose tragic twists
Try modern nerves, appease your emulous rage
On the limp substance of the living age,
But touch not ye the antique marble.   Chill
To your embrace, and unresponsive still,
Its firm long-frozen grain will foil for ever
The feeble fierceness of your fangs' endeavour.
For, O ambitious snakes ! tho' snakes you be,
You are not snakes of Tenedos : nor we
Laöcoöns ; nor the wrath you represent
The wrath of an Apollo.   Be content
To writhe in elegiac ecstasies
Round subjects fitted to your strength and size.
Feed on fresh food.   But seek no second feasts
From the old Sun-God's long-since-perisht priests.

VI.

A PROVISION FOR LIFE.

A PINE-TREE bless'd its favour'd fate, because
Room to grow barely 'twixt the grudging jaws
Of one of the chapt sandstone's gravell'd flaws

It found : where early chance had cast its lot
On a bare rock, with leave to thrive, or not,
As later chance might choose, in that chill spot.

" Ah, what good fortune !" sigh'd the grateful tree,
" That in this fissure the wind planted me !
But for its inch of earth, what should I be ?"

Fool ! Thy good fortune was not the bestowing
Of that scant handful of earth's overflowing.
It was—and is—thy faculty of growing.

To E. L.,

WITH FABLES VII. AND VIII.

FAIR soul, that o'er mine own dost shine
  So fair, so far above,
Dear heart, that hast so close to mine
  The home of thy true love :

Be thine these songs of Far and Near !
  Two worlds their sources are:
Each makes the other doubly dear,
  The near one and the far.

VII.

THE BLUE MOUNTAINS; OR, THE FAR.

PART I.

1.

WHEN little kings, whose race was run
  A little while ago,
Had little thrones to sit upon,
  And little else to do,
Within a little town, remote
  From Europe's larger scenes,
There dwelt a man of little note,
  Who lived on little means.

2.

A man, he was, of humble birth and mind,
  His life was lowly, small was his estate.
Yet was there ever a human life confined
  In bounds so narrow by ungenerous fate,
But it had in it something far and strange?
  This man, from youth to age, had lived and grown
In a great longing for a far blue range
  Of hills that hover'd o'er his native town.
Ne'er had his footsteps climb'd those mountains blue,
  But half his life, and all his thoughts, dwelt there.
He was a man beyond himself. They drew
  His being out of him, and made it fair.
For wheresoe'er his gaze around him roved,
  There were those beautiful blue hills. And he,
Who lived, not in himself, but them, so loved
  And so revered them, that they ceased to be
To him mere hills, mere human feet may wend.
  Their azure summits, to his longing view,
Were features of a dear, though distant friend,
  In kingly coronal and mantle blue.

3.

And " Oh," he mused, " full sure am I
Those mountains feel, in silent joy,
The love my gaze doth give them. They
Seek it, indeed, with signs all day ;

Down drawing o'er their shoulders fair,
This way and that, soft veils of air,
And colours, never twice the same,
Woven of wind, and dew, and flame,
And strange cloud-shadows, and slant showers.

" That is their speech.   'Tis unlike ours,
Easy to learn, tho', if one tries ;
One only has to use his eyes.
The colours are the vowels.   These
Are liquid links whose mobile ease
Such fluent combination grants
To those substantial consonants,
Precipitous crags, and sudden peaks.
The accents are the lightning-streaks
And thunder-claps, that render, each,
Such emphasis to mountain speech.
Next follow fog and mist, which are
Verbs we may call irregular ;
Perplexing when at first you view them,
But persevere, and you'll get thro' them.
Then comes the rain, which just supplies
The necessary quantities
Of notes of admiration.   Far
Too many, folks may think they are.
But if such folks could understand
The mountains, there on every hand
They'd find about them more, far more,
Than notes of admiration, score

On score, suffice for.   Think, what lands
And peoples every peak commands !
Then find the statesman that knows how
To govern one land.   As for two,
That task's beyond the best, we feel.
Now, had we, like the hills, to deal
With winds, and storms, and clouds, and snows,
Nor lose our dignified repose,
Who'd wonder why the hills abound
In thoughts so serious, so profound,
About what men, when met together,
Talk, without thinking, of—the weather ?
But still to talk it is men's wont,
Both when they think and when they don't.
Ah, good old hills !   If Majesty
Should, some day hence, be forced to fly
From all her other thrones on earth,
'Tis there, with you, who gave her birth,
That she her latest home would find,
Above, but still *among*, mankind !"

PART II.

1.

Thus ever the fancies of the man
(Like their own restless rills)
Upon the mighty mountains ran,
Refresht by far-off hills.

Not one of his neighbours, he could swear,
Half so well as those mountains, knew him,
Who wrapp'd his soul in their robe of blue.
And, if that were fancy, *this* was true :
That, whether or not, those mountains fair
For the good of this man had a thought or care,
Much good they had contrived to do him
By simply being there.

2.

His only wish was to tell them of it,
And requite them for it.   But not, as now,
When to every peak, with the snow above it,
And the azure of heaven above the snow,
It was only his wishes that found their way ;
But among the hills, *himself*, some day
Before he died, if that might be,
When the hills could hear what he had to say,
And how much to say to the hills had he !

3.

O heavenly power of human wishes !
For as wings to birds, and as fins to fishes,
Are a man's desires to the soul of a man.
'Tis by these, and by these alone, it can
Wander at will thro' its native sphere
Where the beauty that's far is the bliss that is near.
Fate favour'd the wishes of this poor man.
For the wave of the ebbing century ran

In a sudden surge of storm at last
Over the little spot of earth,
Where, else, unnoticed he might have past
To his obscure death from his obscure birth.
And thus he, whose life had lain out of sight,
A social nothing, the strain and swell
Of the time's strong trouble swept into light,
And suddenly made perceptible.
Then, as soon as noticed by those in power,
The man was honour'd (O happy hour !)
By the sight of his name in a Royal Decree ;
Which inform'd the world that he (poor *he !*
Who could have fancied so strange a thing?)
Had really and truly lived to be
A cause of alarm to his lord the King.
For it banish'd him to a place, he knew
Must be in the midst of those mountains blue.
And thus his wishes, at last, came true.

PART III.

1.

Glad was our friend, when himself he found,
In travelling trim, to the mountains bound !
The way was long, and the road was steep,
And, before he had got to his journey's end,
The night was dark, and the hills asleep.
" Aha !" thought he, " will they know their friend,
Who is here at last ?   Too late to-night

To see them, of course !   They are sleeping now.
But to-morrow, to-morrow at earliest light,
I shall arise ere the red cock crow,
And visit mine old friends, every one."

2.

So, at dawn, he arose with the rising sun,
And forth, as blithe as a bird, went he.
At first he was puzzled and pain'd, to find
All round him a field which appear'd to be
Just like the fields he had left behind :
A little meadow of grass, hemm'd round
With many a little hillock and mound,
Which hinder'd his sight from ranging far.
" But soon are these small hills climb'd," he thought,
" And behind them, doubtless, the blue ones are,
Where, sportively hiding, they wish to be caught."

3.

Then he mounted the hillocks that rose close by,
And thence, indeed, he beheld once more
The old blue hills.   But they were not nigh ;
They were far, far, far away, as before.

4.

" Strange !" he mused, " yet I travell'd all day,
Ay, and more than the half o' the night, too, post !
And all my life I have heard folks say
That the blue hills are but a day, at most,

From my native town.   Did they err, I wonder?"
Then, he ask'd of a traveller passing by,
" Pray, sir, what is that country yonder?
There, where the hills are so blue and high."
And, when the traveller had told him the name
Of the place where the blue hills now were seen,
Alas, poor man ! 'twas the very same
Where, till then, he had all his life long been :
The country about his native town—
His birthplace—whence he had just been banish'd.
The blue hills *there* he had never known,
And the blue hills *here*, which he loved, had vanish'd.

PART IV.

1.

" And have I been living, then, all this while
In a blue land—really and truly blue?"
The exile sigh'd with a sorrowful smile,
" And never dream'd of it?   Can it be true?
Never dream'd of it !   All seem'd grey,
Or dusty white, with a patch or two
Of lean green grass, or raw red clay,
To enliven the rest.   But blue?... blue?... blue?"

2.

And the man fell into a reverie.
O'er his cerulean home a brood
Of etherial clouds was floating free.
And they sign'd to him, and he understood.

3.

" As the waves that are clad in the azure of ocean,
    So clad in the azure of heaven are we.
As thou movest, we move, with an unseen motion ;
    And, where thou followest, there we flee.
For the children of Never and Ever we are,
And our home is Beyond, and our name is Afar.

" Never to us shall thy steps attain,
    Nor ever to thee may we draw nearer.
But, if fair in thy vision our forms remain,
    Still love us, the farther we are, the dearer,
And be thou ours, as thine we are,
For what were the near, were it not for the far ?

" Look above, and below—to the heaven, the plain !
    The low and the level, they disappear.
The aloof and the lofty alone remain.
    And, for ever present tho' never near,
Whilst ours are the summit, the sky, and the star,
Still thine is the beauty of all that we are."

4.

All this, in his much-loved mountain-tongue,
The man's heart, hearing it, understood.
And he thought of the old old days, so young !
But he spake not : only, let fall a flood
Of passionate notes of admiration,
Over his wan cheek silently sweeping.
As when, in their sorrow and desolation,
At the death of the summer, the hills are weeping.

5.

Then the folk about him, who knew not aught
Of that mountain language, shook the head.
" How he taketh his sentence to heart !" each thought.
And "Courage ! the times must mend," they said.

VIII.

A WHEAT-STALK; OR, THE NEAR.

I.

THE cattle tinkle down the lanes,
　And there the bramble roses blow.
From rocky haunts to reach the plains
　The rills, with shaken timbrel, go,
　　　Gay dancers light!
　　　The hills are bright
With gleaming peaks of golden snow.

By fragrant gales in frolic play
　The floating corn's green waves are fann'd,
And all above, broad summer day!
　And all below, bright summer land!
　　　And, born of each,
　　　Far out of reach,
Those shining alpine spectres stand.

II.

A world of beauty, grandeur, grace,
　　Abundance, fill'd with force divine,
No sooner doth mine eye embrace
　　Than my soul hath made it mine.
　　　　How deep, O soul,
　　　　　　Thy depth must be,
　　　　　To hold the whole
　　　　　　Of a world in thee !

III.

But O eye, and O soul, is your thirst yet sated ?
　　Or what more do ye claim for your own ?
Must this world, at the best, be so lightly rated,
　　For the sake of a better, unknown ?

Ah, farther away than the farthest hill-top
　　Do I *feel* mine own boundless emotion !
And my heart, tho' o'erbrimm'd it may be by a drop,
　　Is contented not with an ocean.

IV.

On the blossomy lattice ledge,
　　Whence, far away, I descry
The long land's light blue edge,
　　With beyond it only the sky,
From a glass half fill'd with water
　　Leans an ear of wheat.   'Tis a prize

Which erewhile my little daughter
　　Brought hither with brighten'd eyes.
Its stem, when she pluck'd it, stood
　　An inch higher than she could see.
And the wheat-field to her was a wood,
　　And this wheaten stalk was a tree.
And, as soon as her gift my fairy
　　Had deign'd to confer upon me,
With a frolicsome footstep airy,
　　Off, carolling, gamboll'd she.

V.

A little child, scarce five years old,
　　And blithe as bird on bough ;
A little maiden, bright as gold,
　　And pure as new-fall'n snow.

Things seen, to her, are things unknown :
　　Things near are far away :
The neighbouring hamlet, next our own,
　　As distant as Cathay !

Far things, which we nor feel, nor see,
　　To her seem close and clear.
In yon blue sky God's guardian eye
　　She feels, and feels it near.

What need hath she, our world should be
　　So wondrous wide and far ?
Such worlds unknown are all her own,
　　And every world a star !

VI.

Why, dreaming ever, clings my gaze so fast
    To this small wheat-stem ? Whence its power to draw
My refluent thoughts from yonder distance vast,
    And hang them on a homely wheaten straw ?

It is that, small and homely though it be,
    This ear of wheat so homely and so small,
Because it is so near, so near to me,
    Hath size enough and power to cover all.
It leans along full twenty leagues of land,
    And hides them with a straw.   The purple hills
Peer through its hoary panicle.   The grand
    Horizon's azure orb one wheat-stem fills.

Kindly perspective !   Little things close by
    Exceed great things remote : for Nature's art
Brings vision to a centre in the eye,
    Affection to a centre in the heart.
And, were it not so, light and love would be
    Lost wanderers ; and the universal frame
A heap of fragments ; and the force to see,
    The force to feel, mere force without an aim.

VII.

O near ones, dear ones ! you, in whose right hands
    Our own rests calm ; whose faithful hearts all day
Wide open wait till back from distant lands
    Thought, the tired traveller, wends his homeward way!

Helpmates and hearthmates, gladdeners of gone years,
　　Tender companions of our serious days,
Who colour with your kisses, smiles, and tears
　　Life's warm web woven over wonted ways,

Young children, and old neighbours, and old friends,
　　Old servants—you, whose smiling circle small
Grows slowly smaller till at last it ends
　　Where in one grave is room enough for all,

O shut the world out from the heart you cheer !
　　Tho' small the circle of your smiles may be,
The world is distant, and your smiles are near.
　　This makes you more than all the world to me.

THE ASS AND THE WAGTAIL.

1.

THE ass began to bray.
All who heard him, by the voice of him affrighted,
Cried " How horrible ! " and turn'd their heads away.

2.

The sun began to shine.
All who felt him, by the beam of him delighted,
Looking up to him, cried fervently, " How fine ! "

3.

An ass his feelings has.
And the feelings of this ass, alas !
Were wounded.
He said, tossing his head,
(And the scorn his speech betray'd, loud bray'd,
Resounded)

" Hee ! haw !

Lighter than straw

On the wind, fools run

After what glitters. The taste of the day !

Sound worth they shun,

Their praises give to the sun's display,

And to me give none.

Ungrateful and frivolous fools, I say !

For, if I were the sun, they would flatter me, they

Who all fly me now. Yet, if I were the sun,

What could I do for them more, I pray,

Than, being an ass, I already have done ?

I should simply have nothing to do but to shine—

Shine, or be seen, 'twould be all as one :

And no great merit in that, I opine,

If one happens to be the sun."

4.

A wagtail nodded his head.

The ass was pleased. " It is plain

Thou hast understood me," he said.

The wagtail nodded again.

5.

" And my voice hath a charm for *thee* ? "

More movements of affirmation.

" Sage bird ! I see we agree."

(Much encouraged, continued he)

" What senseless exaggeration
In this praise of the sun !   Nay, nay,
I am not unjust, I trust.
I admire, and enjoy, in its way,
(Tho' the end of it all is dust)
The sun's superficial display,
—When there's shadow elsewhere in store.
For what is light without shadow ?
And the sun hath no shadow at all.
When he sprawls all ablaze on the meadow,
One is driven for shade to the wall.
Now, that is the fault I deplore.
True art enjoins exclusion ;
What artists call ' the file.'
Superabundant diffusion
Is the vice of a vulgar style.
The rich are prodigal rarely.
There's some fire in the sun, no doubt.
But of art . . . well, seeking it fairly,
Not a symptom can I find out.
If the least little leaflet green
Chance to cover the finest peach,
He passes it by unseen,
As tho' it were miles out of reach.
Many a statue fair
Of marble god and goddess,
Perfectly Greek, and bare
Of even a bit of a boddice,

He leaves in the damp and cold
Of their grottoes, and groves, and springs,
To gild, in the dust, with his gold,
The commonest insect things.
Is that worthy work (now own !)
For a star to whom it is given
To saunter all day up and down,
Staring about him, in heaven ?
Look at me, little bird !   I am far
From comparing my humble powers
With those of that profligate star.
But, to perfect them, all the twelve hours
I've a practical occupation.
Without it, I care not a whit
For brilliant imagination.
And I value not genius or wit,
If it lacks the elaboration,
The earnest moral tone,
And genuine consecration
Of work—work, steadily done.
'Tis with pride that I bear up and down
Sacks of corn to the mill,
And sacks of flour to the town.
For, whilst useful to others, I still
Feel that fairly and fully mine own
Is the honour on me conferr'd
Of the right to be thus employ'd.
'Tis a privilege, little bird,
By the idle never enjoy'd."

6.

At every boastful word
The ass thus solemnly said,
As tho' in its truth he concurr'd,
The wagtail nodded his head.

7.

And the ass resumed.   " No doubt,
The fat paddock is not for me.
The spruce garden where cabbages sprout,
'Tis but over the wall I see.
From the corn-bin I get not a bite :
To the pampering oat I'm a stranger,
And the fragrant hay is quite
Out of reach of my modest manger.
But of no such dainties I dream.
The thistle, that hardy relation
Of the sickly artichoke,
I have learn'd to know and esteem,
And I relish my well-earn'd ration,
Not envying sumptuous folk.
Then, is it not hard, I ask,
When my voice I raise
In vigorous lays of praise,
To celebrate Virtue's task,
And her days
Well spent,—yon fools, who bask
In the sun's mere casual rays,

All stop their ears with a cry, and fly
My discourse at the very first minute,
Nay, almost before I begin it,
As if the devil were in it ?
Why do they do that, why ? "

8.

Had this worthy ass been content
With the wagtail's tacit assent,
We should never have known, alas !
What a wagtail thinks of an ass.

9.

But he,
Impatient, as well he might be,
After so long saying his say,
Of getting to all that he said
The self-same nod of the head
In for ever the self-same way,
Began to demand of his auditor
An opinion more in detail
Concerning the cause he was pleading for.
Then, the wagtail hopp'd from his rail,
And hopp'd on to a stone, that stood
Half out of the brooklet's bed,
And replied, " Not a word have I understood
Of all that you just now said."

10.

" Not a word ? " exclaim'd the ass, much surprised,
" Not a word of all I said and all I meant ?

And yet, surely, if an ass may trust his eyes,
To each word of it you nodded me assent."

11.

" Nodded," said the wagtail, " ay !
But nodded you assent, friend, nay !
If I nodded 'twas because it is my way,
And because I am a wagtail, I.
So the sun shines, yonder, up on high,
Just because he is the sun.
And so you, too, as you say,
Fetch and carry sacks all day,
Getting thanks for it from none,
Just because you are an ass."

12.

Then the wagtail flew away,
Thro' the trees, across the grass.
And this fable is done.

X.

THE MISANTHROPE AND THE BIRD.

ONE more Alceste, by all the world betray'd,
And overburden'd with unnumber'd wrongs,
The victor vices in their hell-pit leaving,
Sought out on earth some solitary spot
For honourable freedom. Scorn of men
Forth drave him, and desire of desertness,
And deep disgust of affectations fed
On fool'd affections, with a sudden force
Hither and thither, till he found at last
A tract of savage, strange, uncitied land,
Forgotten like himself. There settled he ;
Far from each false Philinthe and Celimène,
And " love unruled by reason," and the troop
Of those " great makers of great protestations "
The world calls friends.

                        This hater of mankind
Walking alone along the windy wold
One morning, spied a falcon in the wind,
That chased a skylark.   And the skylark fled
For shelter to the bosom of the man.
Who, muttering "Miserable little bird,
I give thee what to me none ever gave,"
His cloak unclasp'd, and to the bird vouchsafed
Welcome in woe and shelter from distress.
Then built a bowery cage; where for a while,
With all, save freedom, that a bird can want,
The skylark, seeming well contented, lived.

Was it the memory of a peril past,
That made the sense of present safety sweet?
Or gratitude for benefits received?
Or but the waning charm of change?   Alceste,
Tho' disbelieving human kindness still,
And earthly blessedness still disbelieving,
Believed, at least, that he had blest this bird
With so much bliss as he by that belief
Still made his own, because he was a man.

So lapsed the season.   Longer wax'd the days
And the nights warmer: till a tremor ran,
Preluding the revival of the year,
Along the leafless boughs.   And, ere it pass'd,
Lo you! like love, that changes life, all round,
Above, beneath, the Spring was everywhere;
Troubling the sleep of Nature with mad hopes.

All things of joy and beauty, long represt,
Broke out in revel, riotously sure
Of May's delirious promise.   From whose mirth,
Pelted with buds, the frowning Winter wrapp'd
His white robe round him, like a minister
Disgraced, that from the uprisen people runs,
And fled, barefooted ; muttering " Motley fools,
That fling a saucy triumph in the face
Of fleeting Power, sing ! dance ! pavilion all
The tipsy tops of yonder swaggering trees
With tassell'd fringe ! on every wanton puff
Of passing wind swing out your banners blithe !
Carpet with squander'd broidery, green and gold,
The dull land deckt for your audacious march !
Break ope earth's hidden treasures ! 'twirl and toss
Your silly tinkling timbrels that proclaim
A world's subversion !   Fools, *I shall return.*"

Then, for the skies the skylark yearn'd : and, mad
With memories which the magic of the Spring
Had changed to hopes, he could no comfort find
In any corner of his corbell'd cage.
But, food by day and sleep by night refusing,
He sent forth little plaintive cries, and beat
With petulant beak and breast the ozier bars
Of his unvalued lattice.   This, Alceste
Beheld, compassionately vext ; and sigh'd
" Thou longest for lost liberty, alas !
The snares of earth, the storms of heaven forgetting,
The chill wind chattering on the rainy wold,

And the hawk hovering in blue ambush high.
A wandering odour on the wakeful night,
A warmer breeze thro' budded thickets breaking,
Suffice thee to efface all sufferings past,
Insensate ! and thou flutterest to regain
Thy persecuting freedom.   Out on time !
Doth Memory carve the records of Mischance
With such a careless or a clumsy hand
That, ere the lazy creeping ivy-twine
Hath time to lace her latest epitaph,
It fades away ?   Ah, were her warning words
But graved on granite, the insensible stone
Would keep unblunted all their biting truths :
But she confides them to the tender stuff
That hearts are made of; and the hot blood there,
Born for betrayal, heals old hurts in haste,
Lest the scarr'd nerve, grown callous, miss the smart
Of sufferings yet in store.   Go, silly bird!
Thou know'st not how that folk, self-styled elect,
Which deem'd itself Heaven's favourite upon earth,
Tho' in the desert half a hundred years
It linger'd looking for the Promised Land,
Is at this hour a wanderer as of old,
The byword of the nations !   Get thee gone,
Truster in promises ! "   He oped the cage,
And forth, in vain admonisht, flew the bird.

Some few days after, near the self-same spot
Where, in the autumn of the bygone year
Alceste had saved it from its falcon foe,

He found the skylark dead. Desuëtude
Of self-exertion, caused by comfort got
Without an effort, had relax'd the strength,
And dull'd the craft, which Freedom needs to bear
The bruising buffets of Necessity.
Unshelter'd cold and foodless hunger found
No friend in liberty. A little heap
Of frozen feathers in the mountain grass
Was all that rested of a vain desire
Wreckt on a sea of promise.
                  Seeing this,
" Heart-breaking Liberty ! " Alceste exclaim'd,
" If we be strong, with stronger than ourselves
Thou dost confront us : and, if weak we be,
In vain thy gifts thou givest us. Yet ah,
Safe-shelter'd from thy harsh embrace, we droop,
And find no joy wherever thou art not."

XI.

FORTUNE AND HER FOLLOWERS.

PART I.

Two friends in search of Fortune once set out
Together.   And, for many and many a day,
Up hill, down dale, and all the land about,
Ever in search of Fortune wander'd they,
Till both were tired.   Then one sat down, and sigh'd,
" Of finding Fortune I begin to doubt,
And fear we may have taken the wrong way.
How say you, friend ?"   The other one replied,
" It seems, indeed, that we have gone astray,
For here of Fortune is no trace, in truth.
But there stands one, may haply tell us yet
Which side to turn.   Look yonder !"   'Twas a youth
Who in the crossway stood where two roads met,
And by the bridle held in either hand
A horse.   Himself was looking eagerly
To right and left, both ways across the land,
And seem'd to wait for some one.   " Holla, boy !
Hast seen Dame Fortune pass this way ?"   " 'Twas she

That bade me here remain (for my employ
Is to obey her) until I should see
Two travellers coming, who would ask for her.
And, by the question ye have asked of me,
My charge, I doubt not, doth to you refer.
To whom, as soon as seen, her orders were
That I should give these steeds, which saddled be
For you to mount.   One steed to each."—" O rare
Good Fortune !" cried the grateful twain.   " Say how
May we our benefactress find ? and where ? "
" Nay," said the lad, " that's more, sirs, than I know.
She bade me say her way lies here and there,
And it is yours to find her."   Now, the two
(Because they could not both together fare
By different ways, and had no indication
On which side Fortune waited) thereupon
Reluctantly resolved on separation,
Each following Fortune his own way, alone.
For at the point where they took horse, the road
Split into two, which from the self-same spot
Led right and left ; and not a sign-post show'd
Which was the road to Fortune, which was not.

PART II.

The first of the twain then gallop'd amain
Till he came to the nearest town.
And there he was fain to throw up the rein
At the first inn door, and get down.

For his horse was tired ; as he was, too ;
And of rest and food they were both in need,
Ere they could their journey again pursue.
So there they waited to rest and feed.
But, when horse and man had their strength renew'd,
They started again, and again pursued
The chase ; tho' in vain ; for thus ever again,
As from city to city they journey'd fast,
With each fresh fatigue there was need, for the twain,
Of a fresh repose and a fresh repast ;
Till the horse fell lame of a double sprain,
And the man had no money left at last.
To prison he must have gone, no doubt,
If his host (surmising he might do worse,
When the man had his reckoning all run out)
Had not taken in payment the founder'd horse.
" Ah, scurvy Fortune !" the traveller said,
" This is what comes at the last, I see,"
(And the poor wretch ruefully shook his head)
" Of running about in search of thee.
Here am I, ruin'd, and half-starved dead !
And what is henceforth to become of me ?"
The host heard this, and " Both board and bed
You may earn, if you will.   Rest here," said he.
" Who works for his bread hath a right to be fed.
And that's better than starving, or stealing, at least.
Take service with me.   And endeavour to be
Of some use now to this broken-down beast
You have used so ill."   Tho' it be but stale,
Sweeter, no doubt, than the bread of the jail

Is the bread that is earn'd.   To his evil case
Our traveller had no choice but submit
With a grieving heart and a grateful face,
And, bitterly earning his daily bit
Of bread, and his nightly truss of straw
(For the moneyless man must work, if he can,
And to jail, if he can't, and that is the law)
The master-turn'd-servant now served, alas,
The brute that had brought him to this sad pass.

PART III.

Time fled.   To the door of that inn one day,
Came, at nightfall, a carriage with horses four.
Wealthy and healthy, good-humour'd and gay,
Did its occupant look.   Never counting the score,
For his supper he order'd the choicest and best
That mine host could procure for so noble a guest;
And, as soon as the landlord had shown him his room,
Enquired if he happen'd to know of a lad
He could recommend as a stable groom.
Said mine host, " Tho' to lose him, your worship, I'm
     sad,
There's a poor fellow here I can well recommend."
Then for Fortune's unfortunate follower (glad
To get rid of him thus) the rogue hasten'd to send.
For he thought to himself " What a lucky chance,
To oblige a man of such station

By the much-desired deliverance
From that beggar's prolong'd starvation !"
But fancy the face of the rascal, when
To his wonder he witness'd those two men
(His great rich guest and his stable boy)
With a cry of recognition and joy
Rush into the arms of one another,
As the first exclaim'd, " O friend ! O brother !
Have I found thee at last ? I have sought thee long.
And how changed, dear friend ! Hast thou suffer'd
    wrong ?"
Mine host would have spoken. But here the door
Was shut in his face, and he heard no more.

PART IV.

What he might have heard, had his wealthy guest
Not lock'd him out that he should not hear,
Was (after the poor man's joy was express'd
At tasting once more in his life good cheer,
And feeling his hand by a good friend press'd)
The admiring question, " But tell me, pray,
Since *you* have discover'd it, favour'd one,
The way to Fortune." " I know no way "
The other replied, " tho' to Fortune alone,
My wealth I owe." " By what lucky chance ?
A lottery ?—or an inheritance ?"
" The latter. That horse which she gave me
Is dead long since, and I am his heir."

" The heir of a horse, friend ?   How can that be ?
The same, to look at, our two steeds were.
Mine 's now but a damaged beast, as you see.
How happens it yours was a millionaire ? "
" Listen.   I gallop'd at first, like you ;
But, perceiving, after a day or two,
That I lost my labour, and, what was worse,
Without filling my belly had emptied my purse,
I began to consider the shortest way
Of simply getting from day to day.
Now, for this mine own two legs would do
Just as well as my horse's four ; and so
' I'll kill him,' I thought, ' and the skin of the beast
Will make me, to still jog on, at least
A dozen stout pairs of shoes ; and they
Will cost me nothing for corn or hay ? '
So said, so done.   My horse I slew.
His flesh for meat to the butcher I sold,
And his tail to a Pacha who, having but two,
Had set his heart on a third.   With the gold
Which I got thereby, a barrow I bought
To carry my merchandise about.
For out of the hide of my horse I had wrought
More shoes than I needed, and all were stout.
These others I sold, and increased my store.
And when my stock of leather was out,
As the folk were still eager to purchase more,
Said I again to myself, ' No doubt
It were better for me, so long as my door
The people with purse in hand importune,

Daily to purchase my wares by the score,
If, instead of still running after Fortune,
And so wearing mine own shoes into holes,
I stay where I am, and provide stout soles
For the feet of the fools who to find her fare
By all manner of ways, a motley host.
Since founder'd horses are not so rare
But what I may get them at no great cost.'
It is thus that at last, having beaten dead,
Without riding one of them, horse upon horse,
I find myself where I am, at the head
Of a flourishing business.   Leather, of course.
So, in search of Fortune not needing to spend
My days as of old, when we sought her together,
I set out, as you see, to seek after my friend.
And, not having lost anything, even leather,
Both the one and the other I now find mine.
So here's to Fortune! and pass me the wine.
For what's mine is yours: and we'll share it now,
Old friend, as to seek it of yore we toil'd
Side by side."   Then the poor man cried,
As his lean cheek flush'd with a grateful glow,
" I thank thee, Fortune! for now I see
That the best of thy gifts thou hast saved for me,
A friend whom thy favours have not spoil'd !"

EPILOGUE

(INSTEAD OF A MORAL).

The Fabulist's a pedant, whose profession
Is, with the plainest most precise expression,

To preach in all ways, unto all mankind,
" Be wise, and good ! " Well for him, if we find
Those speaking contrasts in his text, which spare
The preacher's pains, and of themselves declare
The preacher's purpose ! Well, if, on his way,
One with its load, the other with its lay,
Emmet and grasshopper do chance to pass,
Or royal lion and ridiculous ass,
Or crafty fox and over-credulous crow !
For contrasts, clear as these, have but to show
Their faces to us; and, as soon as seen,
All's understood. Moreover, men, I ween,
Without resentment, nay, with laughter glad,
First see their foibles when they see them clad
In fur and feathers, or in hoof and hide.
But ah ! not always doth kind Chance provide
Such fortunate occurrences to him
Who pries not only into corners dim
For secret treasures, but in field and street
Questions whatever he may chance to meet ;
And often for an answer waits in vain,
Or gets one he is puzzled to explain.
So aid me, Gentle Reader ! Staff in hand,
And nose in air, I roam thro' Fable Land ;
And sniff the passing wind, and tap the ground,
Ready to seize on all that's to be found ;
Keen as a sportsman who, with bag and gun,
In search of game goes beating, one by one,
The bushes all. My prey escapes me not.
But this time there falls only to my shot

A moral tale—too moral thro' and thro'
It may be, for a moral tail thereto.
Naught do I scorn, but all that comes I greet.
And, even as swallows, when the air is sweet,
And Spring's abroad, flit swiftly to and fro,
Come and then vanish ere a man cries "lo!"
So flit these fables, a wing-woven mist,
Before the fancy of the fabulist.
This came, as came the others; on light wing
Swiftly appearing, swiftly vanishing,
'Twixt two unknowns.   I caught it as it past.
"O swallow, swallow, since I hold thee fast,
Tell me thy secret ere I let thee go!"
Thus ever hath it been my wont to do
With these light-wingèd visitants from far,
And sometimes long delay'd their answers are.
But this was in a hurry to be gone,
And answer'd quickly, "Secret have I none.
What can I tell thee which thou dost not see?
Two wings hath Fortune also given to me,
Which now are fluttering to be far away.
Loose me, and let me use them while I may!"
Surprised, I loosed the bird.   Away it flew.
And with it fled away the moral too :
Dropping this counsel, as I watch'd it flit
Like Fortune's self—not to run after it.

XII.

COMPOSURE.

1.

SEAWARD from east to west a river roll'd,
Majestic as the sun whose course it follow'd,
Filling with liquid quiet of clear cold
The depths its husht waves hollow'd.

2.

No wrinkle ruffled that serene expanse ;
Till, percht atiptoe on its placid path,
A tiny rock the surface pierced by chance,
Whereat it foam'd with wrath.

3.

Over the depths, indifferent, smooth of pace,
The current with continuous calm had crost.
Yet lo, a little pinscratch in the face,
All its repose was lost !

XIII.

SIC ITUR.

1.

BEHOLD yon sleep-soft phantom opaline
(That seems " such stuff as dreams are made of ") rise
And wane, as dreams do from awakening eyne,
Above the woodman's hut.   Like one that tries
Uncertain paths, from prison precincts flying,
The frighten'd spectre pauses, turns, and stoops ;
Confused, unused to freedom ; faint, fast dying.
The breath of liberty descends on it
Fierce as a brigand from his ambush swoops,
And, cowering, see the brow-beat craven flit
Along the tops of the tumultuous trees !
There, pallid patches of its shroud, all torn,
Float, feebly tossing on the fitful breeze
That heaves about these forest haunts forlorn,
And with low mocking laughter murmurs " Lost ! "
As fades in film the desultory smoke.
But would ye learn what life hath lived this ghost ?

Listen! for now the wind is in the oak,
Its weary chronicler.

2.

But yesterday
'Twas the fairest child of the Forest green,
From whose waving arms she now wanes away,
A bodiless goblin.   Safe, unseen,
The sleek-limb'd hart in his slumber lay
At the foot of her, gladden'd with grassy shade
When the glaring wave of the noon wash'd clean
All shadow away from the open glade.
And the birds, that had dream'd in the far-off lands
Of a life to be lived in her leafy boughs,
And had travell'd by night in seafaring bands
Over the ocean to meet and carouse
Here in their fair predestined home,
Blithe music made from her dancing dome.
And the squirrel, that bird who, instead of wings,
Hath a spirit within him that soars and springs,
Set her fluttering spray in a tremble sweet
As the tender tremour that mounts and moves
Through the limbs of a maiden whose pulses beat
'Neath the first light touch of a hand she loves.
And the wind, that gossip so indiscreet
(The confidant of the unconfiding)
Ever at eve, when the high day's heat
Was calm'd and cool'd, thro' her branches gliding,
Whisper'd low to the listening wood

Secrets, echo'd from tree to tree,
Yet by none of his listeners understood ;
For the pleasure alone, as it seem'd to be,
Of betraying the trust received from many,
Without wrong done to the faith of any.

3.

Art thou weary of wandering
About a noisy world alone ?
With plumage soil'd and broken wing
Fly to the Forest, weary one !
For there is the City of Refuge fair,
Where Silence and Repose,
Two lovers banisht the earth elsewhere,
Dwell safe from a world of foes.
But unloved was the Forest's restful lot
By the Forest's child who had wander'd not.
The far-off clouds as they wander'd by
She watch'd, and felt with a wishful sigh,
" I would that a wandering cloud were I !
To follow the sun o'er the azure deep,
And catch the last kiss of the dying day,
And bear in my bosom the moon asleep !
With the winds of summer to sport and play,
With the snows of winter from steep to steep,
Wrapt in a mystical mantle grey,
To mount, and pause o'er the world, and peep
At my pictured self in the pools, and stray

Over wide waters and over broad downs,
Windy sea-beaches and turreted towns,
Clothing myself in all hues that be,
And taking all forms that seem fair to me;
To dream, and create what I dream of, too;
Float, a white feather thro' fathomless blue;
Fly, a wing'd dragon, with plumage of flame
Lurid and purple, strange news to proclaim
Of the Storm that is plotting to levy wild war
On the pines, whose tall people his progress bar.
Then bathe, a bright naiad, at eve, bosom bare,
All rosy with rapture, in wells of warm air
By the waves of the sunset bequeath'd as they sink,
For the baths of my beauty, on Ocean's brink;
And thro' moonlight and midnight to melt out of sight
In the depths of the heavens like a dream of delight!
Ah! dream of delight that dissolves even now!
For, fasten'd here to the earth below,
My fingers clutch but the sordid ground
To whose chill lap is my sad life bound.
Lost in the crowd of my neighbours, far
Lonelier thus than the lonely are!
Divining all, and beholding naught
Save that which escapeth as soon as sought;
Seeing only the clouds sail by,
Hearing only the stray winds sigh,
Embracing those that, embraced in vain,
With a careless chirrup depart again.
Wretchedest life! ah, when will it end?"

4.

It ended then.   Death came to befriend
Life's longings.   A stroke of the hatchet . . . one—
Two—three . . . and that unloved life was done.
With a sigh, then a groan, did the tree sink down,
Beating the air with her branches.   Blown
About her, leaflets like drops of blood
Sprinkled the sod.   On the torn soil stood
But a stump deform'd, like a block that awaits
Some victim dragg'd from his dungeon gates
There to perish.   Nought else remain'd
Of the life that had been by itself disdain'd.

5.

Woodsmen and headsmen—doomsmen all—
Are quick at their work.   'Tis a word and a blow.
And that word is a word by the axe let fall,
Stopping life's prate.   For from ages ago
Between iron and life is a rancour old,
And the iron emergeth again and again
From the earth's black bowels, his birthplace cold,
Only to bite, and shed blood, or give pain.

6.

What did the woodmen want?   No more
Than fuel to boil their broth.   Not so
The iron, whose rancorous soul was sore

For the want of a victim to fell and lay low.
And for ever, as long as the years roll by,
Shall such fellowships in another's woe
(The alliance of Spite with Stupidity)
Be able, as this was, to overthrow
Something beautiful, something high,
Or something that sought to be both,
And seem'd born for a fairer fate
Than to boil Vulgarity's daily broth
On the fire that is fuell'd by Hate.

7.

The Tree to the clouds did aspire :
The Axe for destruction panted :
The Woodmen wanted to fuel their fire :
And they all of them have what they wanted.

8.

In ghastly cloud the ghost of the dead tree,
Finding an issue from the roof, arose
And, o'er its native forest floating free,
Beheld that ancient City of Repose
Where it had lived and dream'd.   Accomplisht now
Both dream and life !   It knew itself a cloud.
Fain to its former brotherhood below
It would have whisper'd from its phantom shroud
What phantoms feel, and only phantoms know.

But their yet green and living leaves grew grey,
Paled by its spectral presence as it pass'd,
And shuddering shrank.　Slowly it waned away
Into the void, invisible at last !
Yet scattering, as it faded, downward flakes
Of sullen soot that o'er the forest fell
Like lost illusions on a heart that aches
When Hope departs and Memory sighs farewell.

9.

Follow, O follow with regretful gaze
Those waning orbs that float and fade between
The earth and heaven, i' the void where nothing stays,
Clouding heaven's azure, shadowing earth's green !
Desires disbodied.　Phantoms.　Promises,
Fraudulent promises which Life hath given
And Death pretends to keep.　Souls of dead days,
Hopes of lost hours : that fade 'twixt earth and heaven !
We rake the ashes that you leave behind,
The sole realities that rest of you,
And there still beggar'd Memory seeks to find
The gold false Hope to feed his sorceries threw.
But even these, some day, the hankering wind
Will scatter in the void, between the blue
We take for heaven, the green that once was earth.
Death's silent answers to the cries of birth !

XIV.

DIOGENES OR ALEXANDER ?

1.

BOHEMIAN born, but by laborious art
To perfect polish smooth'd in every part,
And form'd to shine with frigid grace, acquired
From that hard lucid style that's most admired,
A Water-Bottle of the last design
Glitter'd among the flowers and dishes fine
That brightly blush'd and proudly beam'd upon
The festive board of some Amphitrion.

2.

New to the place, he gazed in pure delight
All round the snowy Saxon damask, bright
With golden garniture, and florid piles,
And porcelain shepherds peeping with pert smiles
From Arcadies of Sevres.   Flatter'd pride
Beam'd out of all his features, as he sigh'd

"O Form! Form! thou art everything! Nor yet
(Beam-bathed and glory-girt) can I regret
That long, laborious, painful preparation
Which form'd me fit for this exalted station.
Yes, Form is everything.   Severe and hard
Its acquisition : but what rare reward
Awaits the acquirer!   Common flint was I,
Who, thanks to Form, now glitter radiantly
As any gem.   O triumph! not in vain
(*Per aspera ad astra !*) was the pain
That polish'd, point by point, and line by line,
This well-consider'd perfect form of mine!"

3.

But, whilst he mused self-laudatory thus,
Ye gods! what sudden object scandalous
And sinister confronts his casual glance?
A valet pour'd the sparkling wine of France :
And in the bottle, gross, ungainly, black,
From which it foam'd he recognised alack,
A long-forgotten cousin.   Sore distrest
For fear this low connection should be guess'd,
The delicate Decanter sigh'd aghast,
"How hath that blackguard turn'd up here at last?
Whence comes he?   Talk of Form, indeed!   O fie,
The clumsy sloven! what vulgarity!
He hath not even wash'd his face, I'll swear,
Nor brush'd his coat. 'Tis cobwebb'd. What an air
Of back-slum unacknowledgeable life!"

4.

If one had struck him with a carving-knife,
No greater shock could have been dealt thereby
To that fine sense of strict propriety
Which made our poor friend, even when in a passion,
The mould of Form and water-glass of Fashion.
Still greater wax'd the wonder of it all,
When neither host nor guests one word let fall
Of passing reprobation or disgust,
As more such shabby upstarts forward thrust
Their necks, and spouted.   To a pitch it grew
When, after each had pour'd libations new,
In ladies' eyes a deeper starlight danced,
More briskly round the rippling converse glanced,
Or sparkled off in spray of laughter light,
The wise grown witty, and the dull grown bright.
And, when at last the spritely feast was done,
And from the board its merry guests all gone,
(The portly Banker-Prince ; the last Prose-Poet,
New to the world though he profess'd to know it ;
The Wit, who had out-dined a generation
Of other wits, who dined for reputation ;
The famous Traveller, fresh from Timbuctoo ;
The last survivor left of Waterloo ;
The year's five Beauties, each in rival trim)
Not one of all of them had noticed him,
Tho' keen observers were they, all and each.

5.

Left to himself (as on a desert beach
A limpet by an ebb'd-out tide) among
The silent sideboard's stationary throng
Of glassy things, he spied an old Carafe ;
Crackt, and so out of service ; but still safe
From the sad fate of commoner crackt glass,
Since sole survivor of a set that was
Beauteous and precious in its time, tho' now
No more the fashion.   And, relating how
His feelings had been shockt, "Dear Madam, deign,"
Said he, "this contradiction to explain."

6.

" Alas ! " the Old Beauty answer'd with a sigh,
" Young friend, none better can do that than I.
O pleasant *petits soupers* of the past !
Wild, wicked, witty evenings, gone so fast !
How unremember'd are their mirth and grace !
'Twas there the rogue was in his natural place,
Whose presence disconcerted you to-night.
'Twas there he reign'd, the soul of all delight
All laughter.   Ah, and those fair dames were sly !
We pour'd them out our pure propriety
In vain.   For form's sake, they vouchsafed three sips,
Returning ever with their pretty lips
To his pert fountain.   Ay, and then, O child,
What fun, what frolic, what adventures wild,

What scandals I have seen, and I could tell !
And all this rascal's doing.   Well, child, well,
Give him his due.   I said, and still I say,
The rogue's a rogue, but in a sort of a way
There's something good in him."   The old Carafe,
Looking like a diaphanous giraffe,
(The *nec plus ultra* of all disproportion
'Twixt neck and body—a sedate distortion)
Said this with such an air as ladies old
Assume when they break off a tale half told,
But leave the purport of it plain enough,
Clinching their last word with a pinch of snuff.

7.

" But," said the novice, growing thoughtful, " why,
Dear madam, is it, then, that you and I,
Whose form is perfect, lack the charm which still
With such sweet influence doth inform and fill
What flows from him who hath no form at all ? "
" Hey !" said the old one, " Man is what I call
The greatest paradox in all creation,
And I can give no other explanation.
One thing he thinks, and does another thing :
Makes money, saves it, and, when saved, doth fling
His money out o' window : ne'er hath found
His best friends out till they lay underground :
Only consults his health when it is gone :
And if he values virtue, I, for one,
Believe he does so simply for the sake
Of vice, which virtue doth by contrast make

More to his taste.   For all his folly flows
From that one drop of wisdom Heaven bestows
In mockery on him for no use at all.
He boasts his elevation in his fall ;
And still, the lower that he lies, the more
He deems his natural place was high before.
Height measures he by depth, seeks peace in strife,
And calls all this the Poetry of Life."

8.

" But," cried the young one, " what has that to do
With our low cousin ? and how, even so,
Does he contrive to make such a sensation ?"
" Child, 'tis a sort of natural inspiration
Which men, who persecute by turns and pet it,
Ignore first, then o'er-rate, and then forget it.
'Tis not worth getting, if it could be got.
As, just investigate the woeful lot
Of those to whom 'tis given, and you'll find.
One bright spark wandering on a midnight wind !
Our friend's a being, call him what you will,
Of genius ; who has simply turn'd out ill,
As genius generally does.   Do you
So envy him ?   That's more than you would do,
Knew you but how, till just an hour before
His recent triumph, which so soon was o'er,
The poor wretch fared.   A dingy outcast he,
Who unobserved, till chance his lot set free,
Lay dark in silence, solitude, and cold.
Such was his past.   His future ?   Oh, soon told !

How fares he now?   Thro' yonder window peep,
You'll see him lying on a loathsome heap
Of stable ordures in the base back yard.
And if his fall, which must have hurt him hard,
Hath not yet shatter'd him, some scavenger,
Raking among the unsavoury refuse there
In search of fallen and forgotten things,
Where blue flies buzz and the rank nettle springs,
Will haply filch him from his filthy lair.
What next?   In some grim garret, Heaven knows where,
Methinks I see our miserable friend
Serving to hold the bit of candle-end
By whose sick, smoky, feeble flame he'll see
Some other genius, badly off as he,
Pouring on paper the portentous proem
Of some sublime unpurchaseable poem.
Another kind of wine-flask, full of froth
Most evanescent!   And the fate of both
Is, trust me, miserably much the same.
A life's discomfort for a moment's fame!
Our lot is better.   Not much use are we;
But folks, at least respect us—as you see."

9.

The young Decanter mused; nor made reply.
Save by an inward meditative sigh;
Which we translate, as well as we are able,
By the famed query which preludes this fable.

XV.

A LEGEND.

"Die Tugend erwartet ihren Lohn in jener Welt; die Klugheit hofft ihn in dieser; das Genie weder in dieser noch in jener : es ist sein eigner Lohn." *—SCHOPENHAUER, ii. 260.

It was the eve of the day
Which for the sake of St Peter
Christendom honours : and he,
Being the Porter of Heaven,
Pray'd St Thomas to take
Charge of Heaven's gate for awhile ;
Since on the morrow himself
Needs must be present in Rome,
There to receive, and reward,
Christendom's praise and its pence.

Prudent St Thomas, however,
Is the most scrupulous, most

----

* Virtue awaits its reward in the next world ; Ability in this ;
Genius in neither.   Genius is its own reward.

Conscientious of saints.
Conscientious, because
He, the Celestial Empiric,
Even in high metaphysics
Follows the physical method,
Experimental, exact;
Judging of things for himself,
Never dismissing a doubt
Till he hath probed it and proved.

Therefore St Thomas refused,
Firmly refused, to take charge
Of the Celestial Gate,
(Lest he should thereby incur
Charge, too, of error—the Church
Holds for a damnable sin)
Save on condition that first
Peter should point to him out
Whom, without risk of himself
Being thereby taken in,
He into Heaven might take.

Peter, tho' firm as a rock,
Knows that a point may be gain'd
Best by not arguing it.
" What!" he replied, "only that ?
Good! since you will, be it so !
Brother, between you and me,
'Tis but a sinecure.   Still,
Better prevention than cure.
Put on your hat.   We have time."

Safe, then, he fasten'd the Gate,
Popp'd in his pocket the keys,
Hail'd the first cloud that came by,
Into it jump'd with St Thomas,
And in a trice the Apostles
Travell'd together to town.

"Now," said St Peter, "observe!
Over their heads who must die
Ere the night's done, you'll perceive
Trembling a little blue star."
"Ay," said the other, and lo!
Everywhere round him he saw
Hanging o'er hundreds of heads
Tremulous little blue stars.

Heeding not any of these,
Peter, however, went on.
Thomas was fain to ask why.
"Oh," said the Porter of Heaven,
"These are no cattle of ours.
Look at them closer, you'll see!"

Then did St Thomas perceive
Station'd in charge of them all
Pert little sentinel imps
Clad in the colours of Hell.

Groaning, he made with his staff
Many a sign of the cross;

Which by those sentries satanic
Was, with a deference mock,
Duly saluted, as on
Through the iniquitous town
Pass'd the two Saints with a sigh.

Reaching the suburb, where sin,
Wedded to misery, tastes
Something of hell upon earth,
There in a hovel they saw,
Stretch'd on a sack of foul rags
Feebly, an old poor man.
Over the old man's head
Trembled a little blue star.

" Brother bear him in mind.
He is," sigh'd Peter, " alas,
The only one of them all
Whom, ere the morrow, in Heaven
Thou shalt receive to his rest.
All that was not in our gift
He upon earth has refused,
Trusting to us for his all.
All we can give him, we owe.

" Therefore the soul of this man,
When it to Heaven returns
Pure as from Heaven it came,
Bear thou, asleep on thy bosom,
Into the meadow of God,

Sweet with the innocent breath
Breathed by the children who died
Pure in the moment of birth.

" Threescore and ten are the years
God to the life of this man
Gave : and to him they have given
Poverty only, and pain.
Now, in the moment of death,
Nothing of him do they leave
Which is not innocent, sweet,
Simple, and pure as the soul
Breathed by the Giver of Life
Into the babe that is born.
Truly he hath his reward.
Now let us go."

                          But " O stay ! "
" Still," said St Thomas, " I see
Two men yonder, and lo !
Hovering over their heads
Tremble two little blue stars.
Yet can I nowhere perceive
Sentry satanic or guard
Set for the souls of those men.
Surely for them there is hope ?

" Yonder magnificent mansion !
Is he the lord of it, he
Who, while the death-star unheeded
Brightens his serious forehead,

Seems to be pondering, planning,
And counting the chances of life?
Life, for the will and the purpose,
Ay, and the lion-like power,
Pent in the brain that makes broad
That man's mountainous brow,
Such life, sure, hath a value
Not to be lost in the tomb?"

" He?" with contemptuous accent,
Shrugging his shoulders, the old
Much-experienced Apostle
Mutter'd in answer, " he
Knows how to shift for himself.
Let him. His wits are his own.
All that on earth was to get
This man hath ask'd for and gotten.
Nothing owe we to this man.

" Ay, 'tis a notable head !
What will he do with it? Brother,
That is not Heaven's affair.
Tell him as much when he comes
Knocking to-night at the Gate.

" Oh, he will come, never doubt !
Come where there's aught to be got.
Eagerly ask for it too.
Such is the way with them all.
Well, let him get what he can,

So as he gets it himself.
Tell him we owe it him not.
Doubtless he hath his reward."

"Good!" said St Thomas, "but wait!
What of the other?   Behold,
There is he, standing alone
High on the brow of the hill,
Wrapt in a glory that streams
Over his form and his face
Fair from the fall of the sun.

"Pale is his forehead and pure,
Deep is the fathomless eye
Fixt on that source of a light
Fading away from its gaze.
Solemn and sweet is the face,
Saintly the mien of that man,
Even as one that regards
Calmly the coming of calm."

Peter had paused.   And he too
Gazed on the man, and was still.
"Well?" whisper'd Thomas, "Reply!
"Him, at the least, I admit?"
Silently shaking his head,
Peter still answer'd him not.

"What!" cried the questioning Saint,
"Heaven, is it grudged to a guest

Who in his soul, as I think,
Hath it already? who seems
One of the few, the elect,
Sign'd by the sigil of God?"

Still, without answering, still
Lost in his own meditations,
Silently shaking his head,
Peter vouchsafed in reply
Only a negative nod.

" Speak !" cried St Thomas. " Explain !
Porter of Heaven, to him
Must I not open the Gate?"

" No."—" What, refuse him admittance ?"
" No."—" In the name, then, of patience,
What must I do, Brother Saint ?
Thomas my name is, not Job."

Sighingly Peter replied,
" Brother, the man will not come."
" Ah," with a gesture of joy
Thomas exclaim'd, " he will live ?"

" Brother, to-night he will die.
Die, when yon sun shall have set,
Die, and the life he hath lived,
Beauteous and bright as the sun,
Shall, with the sun, pass away.
All hath that man in himself :

All, and he knows what he hath :
Knows it, and asks for no more.
He is himself his reward."

" Nay, then, what is he, my Brother ?
Name me that forehead, those eyes ! "

Then did the holy Apostle
Stretch, with a gesture fraternal,
Forth to the man on the mountain
Solemnly his right hand :
Waving a mute benediction
Whilst, in the ear of the Saint
Who to him listen'd in wonder,
Softly he whisper'd these words :
Words which all Nature receiving
Echo'd with answering thrills :

" That which hath all in itself,
All without any condition,
All without any restriction,
What can it want or demand ?
Having within it, and feeling,
Comprehending, enjoying
All things, nothing is left it,
Nothing, to ask or to get.

" Three men are call'd out of life.
One shall be welcom'd above,
One be lamented below.

Pure was the life of the first,
Potent the life of the second.
Each was an effort rewarded :
One its reward hath in Heaven,
One its reward upon Earth.

" Not so the life of the third.
There is no effort in this,
Therefore for this no reward.

" Man, it was, named the creation.
What was the name of it, think you,
Ere man himself had a name ?
Here is the Thought that created
Finding itself in creation,
Feeling and knowing itself,
And in that knowledge rejoicing.
GENIUS men call it on earth."

XVI.

THE RAINPOOL.

PRELUDE.

1.

THE water flows, and it never stops.
    And the water is many, although it is one:
One made up of innumerous drops,
    Each with a life to itself alone.
And the life of them all is the life of the sea;
    Which is but a drop no longer single,
When, being socially-minded, he
    With his brother drops doth move and mingle.
    For, fling but a poodle in it, and lo!
    When he shakes himself, as a dog will do,
How many and merry the drops reappear!
    Yet each, meanwhile, tho' you were not able
To see him, was there, in his own small sphere,
Busy and brisk.   Let who will give ear
To this (what is it?) that drops from me,
Dropt, to find—whatever that be—

Its fate in the world : a tale—a fable—
A truth perchance—but I know not what.
And, if my fable share the lot
Of its little heroes, and fall forgot,
What matter? It is but a drop in the ocean,
As they were once. With an unseen motion
  Hovering hid in the happy air,
  Social wanderers next they were.
Till, lured through the azure heats aloft
By the wooing sun, so strong, yet soft,
And then caught by the cold of the upper heaven,
    To the realms afar,
    Where the polar star
Hath his palace of ice, these drops were driven.
    There, chill'd by the power
      Of the north again,
    In a resonant shower
      Of riotous rain
A whirlwind chased them over the main ;
    Till, mad with mirth
    To have reach'd the earth,
They leapt, when their need of escape was sorest,
    Down on a Pomeranian forest ;
Rattled his wrinkled oak-leaves shrill,
And made his deep glens hiss and thrill.

2.

Some of them fell in the soft moss under,
And lay there a-quiver with glad bright wonder :

Till, forced to shun the importunate sun,
Thro' the spongy soil their way they worm'd
Into a Secret Society, form'd
Of operative springs.   By these
  With welcome somewhat cold and chary,
Tho' waxing warmer by degrees,
  As merely members honorary
They were elected.   But, in course
  Of time, their due probation o'er,
Each to the rank of a mineral source
  Promotion gain'd; and gather'd store
  Of mineral salt and mineral ore;
Purgative, stimulant, sedative, tonic;
  Then, travelling about on their own account
With sulphur, or iron, or acid carbonic,
  They founded many a famous fount,
Made their fortunes, and all fared well,
At Carlsbad, Vichy, or Aix la Chapelle.

3.

Some of them fell on the mountain flanks;
  Leapt into the first fresh torrent they found,
And, down to the valley in vigorous ranks
  Gambolling, sprang with a buoyant bound
    Over the wheel of the water-mill;
  Whirl'd the reluctant monster round,
    And set themselves with a blithe good will
    To the sawing of wood: then wander'd, still
  And serious, into the lower sluices;
Whence, putting their strength to social uses,

They carried down to the busy town
Many a barge-load's heavy weight
Of flour, and timber, and chalk, and slate,
And . . . But you must not expect me to state
Every detail, or my breath would fail
Before I am come to the end of my tale.
Suffice it to say, that day by day
They did their duty, work'd their way,
In this world's business took their share,
And earn'd their wages, whatever those were.

4.

But the others? They whose lot
Lured me first to tell this story?
Undiscover'd drops, that got
Neither gain, nor grace, nor glory,
How fared they?

5.

In a showery spray,
Brisk as emmets, and as many,
Fast they speeded, unsuspicious,
Down each wrinkle, chink, and cranny
Of the tree they chanced on. "This"
Thought they all, nor thought amiss,
"Is the road most expeditious."
Ah, most expeditious—yes!
To what end, tho'? Who can guess,

Who declare, the end of any
Road that earthly travellers wend?
Even the end of this, my fable,
I to tell you am not able
Until I have reach'd the end.

PART I.

That tree's brown roots, like bronzen snakes that bind
    Some Fury's formidable brows, had wrought,
And rampired deep from reach of sun or wind,
    A dismal pit, where those poor drops were caught.

The cloud was emptied, and the storm was gone;
    The heavens all stainless, and the forest still.
The water, wondering, to itself, alone,
    Whisper'd, and sigh'd with a regretful thrill,

" Was birth a snare, then? and is life a lie?
    And is this all that we were born to be?
Where are the waves, and where the winds? Ah, why,
    Why have we loved and lost them?   What are we?

" What is the meaning of this passion, fill'd
    With pining memories of the infinite tide,
If here forever, straighten'd, stain'd, and still'd
    Thus to a stagnant pool, we must abide?"

There was no answer—save the want of one.
    Silence, obscurity, and solitude!

Scarcely a gleam from the leaf-hinder'd sun,
  Thro' the dense umbrage of that gloomy wood:

Scarcely a sound, save of the fleeting roe,
  Or the faint flutter of some vagrant bird:
No change: no choice: no happy come-and-go:
  Naught to be seen, and little to be heard.

But, in their season, swarms of stinging flies,
  That claim'd that lonesome lakelet for their own,
There laid white egglets; whence anon did rise
  Little red worms that wriggled up and down.

And, once, a headlong acorn, misbegotten,
  Splash to the bottom of the pool did drop,
Like a dead body, blacken'd, swell'd, wax'd rotten,
  Burst, and again upfloated to the top.

Also, an old toad hobbled to the brink,
  And squatted there; so still, she might be dead,
Save that her small black eyes at times did wink,
  And, winking, sparkle in her spotty head.

PART II.

For months and months that melancholy toad
  (Wrapt in profound and sombre reverie)
Her loathsome presence on the place bestow'd.
  Eftsoons! sole mistress of the place was she.

For neither buck nor doe did ever come,
  Nor any bird, to drink of that dark pool.
But gnats around it swarm'd with sullen hum
  At noontide: and at evening, in the cool,

Leaflets, above it, babbled to the breeze,
  Babbling about some business of their own;
A vague monotonous murmur, hard to seize,
  Of many voices, in a speech unknown,

Full of mistrust and mystery; nor aught
  The little pool could understand of it.
Deep in its own dark bosom a dull thought,
  Brightening at moments ere it faded, lit

With vexing visions of a grandeur gone
  The water's stagnant gloom.   In dreams again
It heard the thunderous billows bursting on
  The wind-blown beaches of the roaring main;

And, fool'd by fancy, felt, or seem'd to feel,
  Once more the rapture of a wandering life,
The chase of cloud and bird, of sail and keel,
  Thro' sea and sky,—bright rest or buoyant strife!

Its *will*, at least, was not unworthy yet
  To roam the rosy coral reefs, and roll
Fantastic shells with briny dewdrops wet,
  Or brilliant seabuds, in a sparkling shoal,

Up slumbrous bays of sunny-bosom'd sands,
 Where plumy palm-groves slope to purple seas
Far in the light of lonesome faëry lands.
 And it recall'd with shuddering ecstasies

A memory of white stars, that did whilome,
 Down from the heaven of the high summer night,
Trembling all over with pure passion, come
 To bathe in its clear calm their splendours white ;

And winds, wild horsemen of the boisterous North.
 Who from their skyey coursers leapt, to seize
And in tumultuous dances whirl it forth
 Over the tumbling and bewilder'd seas.

PART III.

And now ? Was all this a delirium, dream'd
 By famisht Fancy ? Had the flimsy hum
Of flies and gnats the sea's deep music seem'd ?
 And was that acorn, floating in the scum,

That bloated acorn, right when she derided
 What to her hollow maggot-eaten husk
The miserable pool with sighs confided
 Of those bright thoughts which thrill'd it in the dusk?

The squelch'd nut counsell'd the reluctant water
 To learn life's lesson of the loathsome toad,

" A sorceress she ! in all the wood none greater :
   Hath roam'd the world thro', and knows many a
      road.

" She'll tell you, nothing is without a reason.
   The flies and gnats (perchance the old toad too)
Enjoy themselves here in the summer season,
   And doubtless fare the better, friend, for you.

" Reflect on that, and be not so dejected.
   Contentment, truly, is the best of things.
We cannot all be all that we expected.
   I, too, have had mine own imaginings.

" And I myself, when I was green and glowing,"
   (The hollow nut said), " I myself, in truth,
Was plagued with whims and wishes.   For my growing
   The heavens then seem'd not high enough ! 'Twas
      youth

" And the green sickness.   ' Why, my pretty Miss,'
   Whisper'd the old toad, ' dream brisk youth away ? '
And introduced me, as you see, to this
   Good lusty playfellow, that's ever gay."

The while she spake, up popp'd, with beaded eyes,
   A fat white worm, self-confident and vain,
Stared at the world with impudent surprise,
   And slunk into the hollow nut again.

" For these, then, am I here ? " dismay'd thereat,
   The wretched pool complain'd.   " For these alone ?
Toadstool and toad, and worm, and fly, and gnat ?
   All for their profit, nothing for mine own ? "

And its face darken'd, and more dismal grew
   Its turbid being ; and a filthy weed
Over its film'd and stagnant surface drew
   Nets to catch sportive spiders ; and a breed

Of brassy-headed, spongy-bodied buds
   Pimpled the slippery banks of that black pool ;
And slugs and snails, dull lazy brotherhoods,
   Lived at their ease there in the gloom and cool.

PART IV.

The Summer smoulder'd into ashes red
   And dim upon the boughs.   Sad Autumn sigh'd,
And, sighing, shook them till they rose and fled.
   Translucent grew the wood's grey roofage wide.

A whirlwind came, and swept the branches bare,
   And in between them widen'd the blue night.
The night was clear and chill.   The wintry air
   Was thrilling; and the stars shone thro' it bright.

Then that forlorn and sullen pool began
   To feel as tho' it were the mystic breath

Of mighty spirits approaching.   Rapture ran,
   Sharp as fierce anguish, thro' the shuddering sheath

By weary Wont and sordid Custom spun
   To hold and hide keen instincts long supprest,
Which now, all tremulously, one by one,
   Leapt to wild life within the water's breast.

For far above it (far, and yet not far,
   Swift-changing to a nearness yet not near)
A sudden glory smote it.   And a star,
   Fall'n in its depths, with throbbing splendour clear

Kindled them all.   And the star whisper'd there,
   "Child of Eternity, despair not thou !
Unenvying, tho' despised, let others wear
   The flaunting robe, and deck the boastful brow

"With the brief diadems of summer days,
   Soon scatter'd by the wind.   Do thou resign
To those that seek it Earth's near-sighted praise,
   Born to reflect Heaven's distances divine !

"Measure thy being's depth by the sublime
   Celestial and immeasurable height
Of what is imaged in it.   Here, in Time,
   (Brief if it be, tho' brief yet infinite)

"Their hour of consciousness arrives at last
   To all the children of Eternity,

Once always, if once only.   Thou, too, hast
    Thy destined hour.   I will return to thee.

" Despair not."   And the image of the star,
    Slowly receding from their surface, left
The conscious waters comforted, as are
    Spirits which, self-discover'd, tho' bereft

Of earthly converse, have held commune high
    Once, if once only, with the heavens above.
Then, while the clear cold of the wintry sky
    Grew slowly solid thro' the frost-bound grove,

Slowly those waters cover'd themselves o'er
    With crystal pall ; whose purifying power
Cleansed all it calm'd and shelter'd till once more
    That promist star return.   To each his hour !

XVII.

CONTAGION.

A BROOKLET, born above a mountain moor,
Down to the level of the world below
Perforce descending, past a dyer's door

Foul with pollution thro' the plain did flow.
The waters of this brooklet from on high,
Still pure and splendid as the spotless snow,

Beneath them could their sunken sisters spy
All soil'd and spoil'd, as when spilt wine doth stain
A pot-house floor.   Whereat they brawl'd out " Fie ! "

A traveller, who had climb'd the hill with pain,
And knew the world beneath it far and wide,
Smiled at the inexperienced disdain

Of those immaculate waters, and replied,
" Wait, pretty fools, until down there you get.
Had they not pass'd the dyer's door, undyed
And white as you would be those waters yet."

XVIII.

AURORA CLAIR.

" Arma habent quia iram habent." *

(The Fabulist offers this fabulous lay
To the Dons that he knows.   No Don Juans are they.)

1.

Shyly shunning the sound and glare
Of the tumultuous thoroughfare,
By black back streets where the moonless sky
In a sallow sluice 'twixt the housetops high
Flow'd, silent save for the distant drum
Of the throbbing town with its human hum,
Its feet that flutter, and wheels that whirl,
Aurora Clair, the weaving-girl,
Walk'd home to her father's house ; where thin
Weak ragged skirts of the town let in
Long rural patches thro' lanes obscure.

* Δια το δυμον εχειν ὅπλον εχει—They have arms because
they have anger.—Aristotle.

2.

Aurora Clair was a maiden pure
Of body and soul, as the Mother Maid
To whom this motherless maiden pray'd
At morn and eve in her chapel small
Of the great grey church, that hath room for all,
The rich and the poor, and the old and young,
The whole year round, and the whole day long.
And in virgin blossom as nobly fair
Of form and face was Aurora Clair
From head to foot as a queen should be,
Tho' only a poor man's child was she ;
Who early and late, with good cheer unchid,
Work'd for bread as her father did.
She at her loom, where she wove and spun
The quaintest creation under the sun,
Wild men with crowns and wild beasts with horns,
Pards, griffins, lions, and unicorns :
He with his chisel and graving-knife,
Whereby he wrought to a wondrous life
Frame and panel, that under his hand
Burst into blossoms of faëry-land.

3.

'Twas the night of the City Saint's Feast Day.
By the side of Aurora all the way
(Proud of his tenth year turn'd) with joy
Ran, merrily carolling, rosy Roy,

Her garrulous, gold-hair'd, bright boy-brother.
The city was swarming, the suburbs were still.
The boy and the maiden took care of each other.
There was nobody else to take care of them. Ill
(To that saint's dishonour) at home in bed
Their father was lying. Their mother lay chill
In the churchyard grass with a cross at her head.

4.

Beauty, Innocence, Feebleness !
In risk and peril these roam by night
Thro' a great town's populous wilderness.
As Aurora found : when with footstep light
The children, to shorten their homeward way,
Cross'd into the great suburban square ;
Which, emptied now of its idlers, lay
In a vacant monotony, all as bare
Of an image responsive to ear or eye
As the silent brain of the fool ; save where
Some Ædile (encouraging art thereby)
Had set up the statue, in bronze bran-new,
Of that famous darling of chivalry,
Who neither fear nor reproach e'er knew.
For which reason perchance, or to save its pence,
The City's Municipal Providence
Vouchsafed not even one lamp, which might
With its humble halo have served to mark
The spot, now dark and deserted quite,
Where the sworded statue stood in the dark.

5.

There, a voice, no Bayard's, as by went she,
The virgin scared.   'Twas the vulgar voice
Of a burly Don Juan who, bold and free,
With speech to the point, and more plain than choice,
His prey pursued.   And the night was late,
The spot deserted, the neighbourhood lone.
Fierce indignation, by fear made great,
Wild cries for help that were heard by none,
Tears, struggles, and prayers,—what avail were they
From the prowler's clutch to release his prey ?

6.

Then Aurora Clair, in her extreme need,
Lifting her looks to the midnight sky
Saw there (as tho' Heaven had taken heed,
And sent him to answer her helpless cry)
Sworded and helm'd, on his stately steed,
The form of the gallantest Christian knight
Of the whole world's gallantest Christian nation,
With his right arm raised as in act to smite.
And, " O Bayard," she cried with the inspiration
Of a sudden hope which that welcome sight
Had awaked in her maiden imagination,
" O Bayard, thou champion of chivalry, thou
Fair saviour of innocence, save me now !"

7.

Hoarse laughter greeted the maiden's prayer.
Not much for statues Don Juans care.
" Too rusty the good knight's sword is grown,"
Her tormentor mock'd, as he touch'd his own.
" But thy champion, pretty one, prithee invite
To supper with us at the tavern to-night."

8.

Scarce had the insolent jest been utter'd
Ere the laugh changed into a howl of pain
And bewilder'd wrath, as the hot blood sputter'd,
Cooling that boisterous boaster's brain.
The arms that were dragging Aurora Clair
Dropp'd; and, as tho' at a god's command,
The brute fell flat on the flintstone there,
Struck in the dark by an unseen hand.

9.

A miracle ! so did Aurora deem ;
Whose only lore being folk-lore old
Had fill'd her with faith in full many a dream
Of faëry and magic and knighthood bold.
And she thought that her champion, arm'd in bronze,
Had really return'd at her invocation
From Elysium, eager to add for the nonce
A fresh renown to his reputation
By rescuing thus from a roisterous churl
That of a poor little weaving-girl.

10.

A miracle?   Truly Aurora was right.
And moreover a miracle, no mere dream,
But a fact of miraculous meaning and might,
A dictating flash of the Will Supreme.
For who is it stands at the maiden's side ?
What second superlative apparition ?
Her own child-brother : but glorified
By the transfiguring intuition
(Never to noble emotion denied)
Of a sudden supreme self-recognition :
Which hath left its flash in the eyes' deep light,
And its pulse in the nostril panting wide,
And its merciless might in the marble-white
Firm lips lock'd fast as a fort defied,
And fists by triumphant intention tight
Clench'd with fate in their fingers fixt.
'Tis an image of awe and of beauty mixt.
For the form of the child is a child's no more,
But a half-god's, hero's, or saint's, of yore ;
Which its own supernatural inward heat
To a supernatural height hath raised.
Even so on Goliath dead at his feet
Might an infant David have gazed.

11.

One moment, swift and yet infinite,
Had reveal'd to Roy, as by lightning-light,

A danger for her whose defender strong
He believed himself, with a pride proved true :
The infernal approach of a nameless wrong :
A deed to prohibit, a deed to do.
Not a moment's doubt ! not a questioning fear !
Once the duty known, are the means not clear ?
Or, the foe being there, is the weapon not here ?

12.

The weapon ! what weapon ? This child, half-clad,
Weak, ignorant—what were the means it had,
What weapon sought it, what weapon found,
For smiting, bathed in his blood, to the ground
That gay cavalier, whose sword at his side
In the starlight shone with a saucy pride ?

13.

Doubter ! learn, then, and understand
There is everywhere, ever, a stone at hand
For the arm that is seeking the means of death.
A philosopher said, and this fabulist saith,
Nature adapts to the use of her lord
The implements that she forges.* Sword

---

* ταδ'οργανα προς το εργον ἡ φυσις ποιει, αλλ' ου το εργον προς
τα οργανα.—For Nature accommodates the instruments to the
work, not the work to the instruments.—Arist.: *De Part.
Animal*, lib. iv. cap. 12.

And shield lack never where'er there be
A soldier ready to use them.　He
Who, having a cause for which to fight,
Hath also courage and will to smite,
Finds waiting for him in pebble or reed
Just such a weapon as serves his need.

14.

Statues we, too, have seen and known.
Irreproachable their renown !
Perfectly polisht in every part,
Models were they of immaculate art.
Noble the names of them, lofty the mien,
Uncontested the fame serene.
Each every pace of his Pegasus knew,
And could pass with applause thro' a classic review
Upon galloping dactyle or spondee sedate,
With the requisite word at the regular rate.
And so, to the pure statuesque in time
Promoted, there they repose sublime.

15.

Well, and good !　But O statues fair,
Why so deaf to our desperate prayer ?
Draw your swords and defend us, pray !
Cannot you hear what the challengers say ?
Quick, to the rescue ! and, undefeated,
Save that importunate maid, maltreated

Much by her modern admirers bold,
Perishing Poësy!   Ah! still cold
And stolid, you stand on your pedestals tall
Solemn, but solemnly helpless all.
Whilst they woo her, pursue her, would fain enjoy her,
But shame her at best, and at worst destroy her.
Feel and be men, then!   The cause of our harm is
That hearts *sine ira* leave hands *sine armis*.

XIX.

LOST TREASURES.

PART I.

IT was the splendid winter-tide.
And all the land was thrilling white,
And all the air was still and bright
With a solemn and songless sunshine wide,
Whose gorgeous uncongenial light
Harden'd whatever it glorified.

And while that glory was streaming amber
Into a childhood-haunted chamber,
A child, at play by the lattice-sill,
Where daily the redbreasts begging came,
Noticed a glittering icicle
That flash'd in the sun like a frozen flame.

So, plucking it off, he seized and put it
Into a box of gilded paper.
There, to be treasured for ever, shut it,
Danced about it with shout and caper,
And then, as a child will do, forgot it.

For suddenly under the lattice roll'd
A music of cymbal and trumpet blent.
And, oh merry and brave it was to behold
The soldiers below, who in scarlet and gold
Marching blithe to the music went.

And after the soldiers, cleaving the cold
Slantwise, shot like a falling arrow,
And perch'd on the sill of the lattice, a bold,
Bright-eyed, sharp-beak'd, hungry sparrow ;
Claiming, with saucy, sidelong head,
His accustom'd alms of a crumb of bread,
Tho' to get what he ask'd he would not stop,
But off, with a pert, impatient hop,
Went twittering over the roof instead.

Next follow'd far more than a man can mention
Of in-door claims on a child's attention.
And at last 'twas a whip to whip the top,
And "Oh, where is Grandfather ? 'tis he must find
    one !"

Then away in a hurry the small feet trot,
Yet pause : for that icicle, first forgot,
And then remember'd all in a minute,
It were surely a pity to leave behind one.

So the treasure-box, with the treasure in it,
Their tiny treasurer carries away.
But ah, what sorrowful change is this

In the box where safely the bright gem lay
Erewhile, a secretly-beaming bliss
To beautify many a winter's day ?

For, drop by drop, is the drench'd box dripping,
And the gilded paper is all undone,
And, away in a shower of warm tears slipping,
The deceitful treasure is well-nigh gone.

So, weeping too, with the woeful story
(In a passion of grief unreconciled
For the lost delight of a vanisht glory)
To the old man hastens the troubled child.

PART II.

Lone by the old hearth was the old man sitting.
He, too, a treasure-box had on his knee ;
And slowly, slowly, like sad snow-flakes flitting
Down from the weak boughs of a wither'd tree,
Fell from his tremulous fingers, wet with tears,
Into the embers of the old hearth's fire,
Wan leaves of paper yellow'd by long years :
Letters, that once were treasures.

                                    The Grandsire
Welcomed the infant with a kind, faint smile.
The burning letters, black and wrinkled, rose
Along the gusty flue ; and there awhile
(Like one who, doubtful of the way he goes,

Lingers and hesitates) along the dark
They hover'd and delay'd their ghostly flight,
Thin sable veils wherein a restless spark
Yet trembled !—and then pass'd from human sight.

How oft had human eyes in days of yore
Above them beam'd, and with what tender light !
Wherefore, O wherefore, had those eyes no more
Upon them gazed for many a heedless year ?
Was not the record which those eyes had read
With such bright rapture in each blissful tear
Still writ in the same letters, which still said
The self-same words ?   Ah ! why not now, as then,
With the same power to brighten those changed eyes ?
Why should such looks such letters meet again
As strangers ? each to each a sad surprise !
" How pale," the eyes unto the letters said,
" And wan, and weak, and yellow are ye grown !"
And to the eyes the letters, " Why so red
About the rims, and wrinkled ?   Eyes unknown,
Nor ever seen before, to us ye seem,
Save for a something in the depths of you
Familiar to us, like a life-like dream
So well remember'd it almost seems true !"

The grandchild weeps upon the grandsire's knee,
And babbles of his treasure fled away.
The old man listens to him patiently,
And tells the child, as tho' great news were they,

Old tales which well the child already knows,
And smoothes his tumbled curls, and comforts him.
The winter day is darkening to its close.
On the old hearth the dying fire grows dim.

PART III.

The child upon the old man's breast was sleeping,
The old man stiller than the sleeping child !
Then slowly, softly, near and nearer creeping
From book-shelves dark, and dusty papers piled,
Old thoughts, old memories of the days of old,
Which lurk'd about that old room everywhere,
Hidden in many a curtain's quiet fold,
Panel, or picture-frame, or carven chair,
All silent, in the silence, one by one,
Came from between the long-unlookt-at leaves
Of old books ; rose up from the old hearthstone ;
Descended from the old roof's oaken eaves ;
Laid spectral hand in hand by twos and threes,
And then by tens and twenties ; circled dim
Around the old man, on whose tranquil knees
Still slept the infant ; and, saluting him,
The eldest whisper'd, " Dost thou know us not ?
Many are we who come to take farewell.
For all departs at last.   Ay, even the thought
Of what hath been.   Sunbeam and icicle,
Childhood and age !   The joys of childhood perish
Before the heats of manhood ; manhood's heats

Before the chills of age.   Whate'er ye cherish,
As whatsoe'er ye suffer, fades and fleets.
What goes not with the heat, goes with the cold.
For all that comes, goes also.   What ye call
Life, is no more than dyings manifold.
All changes, all departs, all ends.   All, all !"

XX.

CHASSÉ-CROISÉ.

A MAN, together in one cage, immured
A lion and a dog.   The dog endured
   Long while a world of drear indignities
From that grim housemate ; who, without the least
Consideration for his fellow beast,
   Stretch'd himself out at ease
In the best places ; while the other lay
Crouch'd in a little corner the whole day,
   And gnaw'd, with furtive tooth, the bones disdain'd
By his strong neighbour, surfeited; dry bones
Gnaw'd bare already.   With reproachful moans
   The poor dog oft complain'd,
And of the human master of his fate
Besought release from wretchedness too great
   For even canine flesh and blood to bear.
But all in vain.   His master heard him not,
Or, hearing, heedless of the creature's lot,
   To change it had no care.

Doubtless far weightier cares weigh'd on him. They
Whose daily business is but to obey
   Must not be suffer'd to exact from those
Who haply rule the house,—or rule the State,—
Attention to their feelings or their fate.
   For what, if some get blows,
While some are pusht on pleasantly? They are
Tools to be used, with no particular
   Consideration for the private feeling
Of either implement—though this, rough-handled,
Mops the drench'd flint—that, delicately dandled,
   Brushes the gilded ceiling,
Fares soft, rests oft, and wears a plumy crown ;
Whilst, soon worn out, the drudging mop is thrown
   To rot, at last, behind the scullery door.
Little do those that use them care, I ween,
For broom or mop, who care but to sweep clean
   The ceiling and the floor.
And, first of all—as touching this dog's lot ;
In all the house there was no other spot
   Half so convenient as that lion's cage
Wherein to stow the dog. In the next place,
The lion served to give a sort of grace
   To the whole house, engage
Attention to it, and make its master's name
Conspicuous : for which reason, it became
   The dignity of that illustrious brute
(Tho', save in this respect, and this alone,
The brute was an entirely useless one,
   And mischievous to boot)

That join'd to him should be some other creature
Of meaner mark, and more familiar feature,
   To show to best advantage all his strength,
And size, and strangeness, and ferocity.   ,
And so the poor dog had no choice, but try
   To bear his fate.   At length
The lord of both on a far journey went;
Leaving, together in the same cage pent,
   The lion and the dog behind him there.
And, in the absence of their master, few,
If any, gave much notice to the two ;
   Who did but poorly fare.
But when the man from his long pilgrimage
Return'd at last, in that neglected cage
   A wondrous change he marvell'd much to find.
For now it was the lion, lean and tame,
That in a corner crouch'd with surly shame,
   And, dog-like, cringed and whined ;
Whilst, stretch'd at stately length in the best place,
The dog, with pride becoming better'd case,
   (His paw upon a bone) the warning range
Of his suspicious and retentive teeth
Did oft, with supercilious growl, unsheathe.
   What caused so great a change ?

MORAL.

There's something of a cur that lurks conceal'd
In every lion : something unreveal'd
   In every dog of spirit leonine.

Long battle with the overbearing power '
Of a brute's senseless selfishness—each hour
   That stretch'd the strengthening line
Of wrongs resisted,—had at last aroused
The something of a lion, nature housed
   In the dog's heart, and made the dog at length
Superior to superiority
Wasted for want of aught its strength to try
   Save one of weaker strength :
As power, meanwhile, by sheer abuse of power,
Degenerating daily low and lower,
   Had dragg'd the lion's nature from above,
Down to that coward something of a cur
Which lurks in every lion's character,
   Like lust, subdued, in love.
'Tis thus that many a small and feeble state,
Striving for justice, hath at last grown great :
   Whilst many an empire opulent and vast,
Down from the eminence, its selfishness
Disgraces, sinking slow to less and less,
   Dwindles and dies at last.

XXI.

A PHILOSOPHER.

PART I.

1.

On a breezy knoll, neither hill nor plain,
But a chance-begotten child of the twain,
In a land of ridges and flats forlorn
Where none went by, save the wind in the corn,
Living the life that beseemeth age
A hermit had chosen his hermitage.

2.

Chosen, it may be, is hardly the word
For a place of abode by fate conferr'd.
But there he was, and he held his ground.
The spot was lone : and the traveller rarely
Paused, as he pass'd it, to gaze around
On the long low fields where the billowy barley
Waved and whiten'd under the wind ;
Or the wolds above where the wandering sheep

Slept and brouzed, and were sure to find
Nothing to do but to brouze and sleep.

3.

Yet, wherever she makes herself at home,
Thought fixes the centre of all creation.
And therefore this hermit, having become
A philosopher, had from his contemplation
Wrought for himself, as the years roll'd by,
A little philosophical system ;
Which explain'd to his own satisfaction the why
And the how he was there ; and so served to assist him
To accept and support with a heart heroic
His lot in life.   Tho', for my part, I,
Not having in me the soul of a stoic,
Had that lot been mine should have surely sought
To exchange it for any less drear and lonely.
For, like the giants Don Quixote fought,
This sage was, in fact, but a windmill only.

4.

A windmill only ?   Monotonous hold
Of weary silence and chill neglect !
Yet a pilgrim tribe hath paid from of old
To this hermit homage of high respect.
For a little people there is, that lives
In the woods and fields, and is loved by all
For the songs it sings, and the joy it gives.
And this sweet folk, whose bodies are small

But whose hearts are large, with religious awe
That weather-beaten windmill saw.

5.

The birds! their ways of living are known,
But who is it knows their ways of thinking?
'Tis true, and 'tis pity, 'tis true, I own,
But truth is truth and forbids all shrinking,
The birds, whatever themselves may call
Their flighty notions, are heathens quite.
Heathens, and not monotheists at all!
But this, tho' of course it is far from right,
Is yet a defect which they compensate
By adoring a number of gods so great
That perchance it comes in the end to the same,
And adoration suffers no loss.
They adore the sun for his friendly flame,
And the freshening shadow that cools the moss,
They adore the bushes, and banks, and brooks,
And the ruin'd towers we men abandon,
And even the low thatch'd eaves, whose nooks
Are as shrines for their household gods to stand on.

6.

What wonder, then, if a windmill be
A demigod to the birds?   For who
But knoweth that four great wings hath he,
Whilst the biggest of birds hath only two?

And a demigod may as well, I aver,
Be a demi-bird as a demi-man.
They deem'd him the bird of Jupiter,
And this tradition among them ran :
One summer morning Father Jove
Created the Windmill, wanting a fan
To cool his Palace Olympian ;
And forbade the celestial bird to move
From the perch assign'd him by Jove's high will.
But, alas for the Windmill ! he fell in love,
Madly in love with the Watermill :
Who then dwelt upon earth. And one dark night,
"Jove never will find me out," thought he,
As earthward slyly he wing'd his flight
To visit the Watermill ; where she,
Like a maiden demure, was sitting beside
Her spinning-wheel. Doth she mourn for him ?
For he, having chosen (not to be spied)
A night when the Moon was wrapt up to the rim,
And, seeing her not as he pass'd on the sly,
Broke one of her horns with a flap of his wing.
The Moon to Jove complain'd, and thereby
All the gods got a gust of the thing,
And the Windmill was banish'd to earth, but still
Far away from the Watermill.
That is the reason he looks so sad.
And the Moon keeps turning her face in heaven,
To hide the scar which that night she had
From the Windmill's wing. He is unforgiven.

7.

Now, albeit their legends admit variation
As to what the Windmill hath been or may be,
In the bird's universal estimation
Some sort of a half-bird-god is he.
And, if for naught else, they would still adore him,
Because of the grains of corn he strews,
For *their* sakes, over the threshold before him;
Where they hold high feast, when they get good news
Of the Miller's mystical visitations.
For is it not Hermes, the herald of Jove,
Bringing the Windmill his daily rations
Of ambrosia sent by the gods above?

PART II.

1.

One day, when the sacred feast was done,
And the others all flown, there remain'd behind
A certain Sparrow, the only one
Of the birds, be it said, whose habit of mind,
From haunting so much the haunts of men,
Hath taken a sceptical turn.   And, when
He perceived that his fellows were gone, said he
To the Windmill, "Listen! It dupes not me,
Thy silence stern, nor thine aspect lonely.
I know thee.   Thou art but a windmill only.

Yet, altho' unduped, I applaud thy plan
For being a god.   Nay, both will and can
Widely encourage the worship of thee,
But I first cry shares, and must have my due.
I am in the secret, as thou may'st see,
Prithee take me into the profit too.
By the profit I mean the sanctuary.
Thou hast in thy belly good store of grain.
A bargain's a bargain.   Why be chary?
Come! let me in.   It will be to thy gain.
I shall keep my counsel, and thine, be sure;
And behave as the priest who is up to the trick
Of the oracle bravely contrived to allure
His flock to the shrine, where their offerings stick.
Moreover, the more grains *I* devour,
The fewer for *thee* to grind into flour."

2.

"Grains, and flour!" the Windmill cried,
"What would'st thou, poor little scavenger?"
But "Marry come up!" the Sparrow replied,
"No bad names, if you please, old sir!
You are but a windmill.   That we know."

3.

The Windmill mutter'd, "I care not how
Nor what I appear to thy bounded ken.
If thy foolishly-twittering folk suppose
That I, too, am a sort of a bird, what then?

Innocent ornithomorphism! Those
Small souls can soar thro' the realm of infinity
To no loftier thought: tho' a mystic sense,
Guessing in me some part of divinity,
Gives them a glimpse of the truth immense.
Men, that are made of a coarser kind,
Careless concerning the causes of things,
In the simple effects of them seek but to find
Their own advantage, and use my wings
For the sake of the grain which I grant they grind;
Then pick up, and prize as precious stuff,
The dust which the voyager, voyaging
To a goal sublime, in his haste shakes off
From the sole of his foot. But this flour, this thing
That you prattle about, I regard with disdain."

4.

Said the Sparrow, flapping a saucy wing,
"What are you there for, if not to grind grain?"

5.

The Windmill sullenly groan'd, "Go to!
Know'st thou the Wind?" "I should think I do!
Who knows not the Wind?" said the bird. "The Wind,
That terrible traveller, hungry and blind,
Whose joy is to ravage and overthrow
Whatever is lofty and great! I know
That he pass'd erewhile o'er mine own house-roof,
Thatch'd so thick I had thought it proof

To the wildest weathers that worry the sky,
Yet he shatter'd it all as he pass'd by.
And I know not yet if I now shall find
The means to rebuild "   .   .   .

6.

        " Whence cometh the Wind ?"
Interrupted the Windmill, stern.
" How should I know ?" said the Sparrow.   "Turn
And look out for thyself when he comes thy way.
And I care not, I, if at home he'd stay,
And not turn other folks out of their home."

7.

Said the Windmill " Learn whence the Wind doth
     come !
The Wind, whose sublime and beneficent nature
Thou fearest, foolish and feeble creature,
Is the brave benefactor of earth and sky.
But who is it giveth him motion ?   I.
And the Wind, at whose whisper the anchor'd ship
Thrills like a bride to her bridegroom's lip,
Were it not for me would, in slothful sleep,
Leave not the lap of the languid deep.
But a single stroke of my sturdy wing
Startles him out of his slumbering.
A second speeds him away through space,
And, fearing a third, he hurries apace

Over earth and thro' heaven, headlong hurl'd
By the strength made mine for the good of the world."

8.

The Sparrow could scarce believe his ears.
After a silence long and perplext
" Friend," quoth he, " since it now appears
From all you say (and who knows what next
You will bid us believe, audacious prophet,)
That the wind is waked by your mighty will,
Give me, prithee, a specimen of it.
See ! not a grass-blade dips on the hill,
Nor a leaf on the lone thorn trees above it.
The time is propitious.   Lift but an arm,
Or wave but a wing, and the wild wind charm."

9.

" The moment is not yet come," unstirr'd
The other replied, and undisconcerted.
" And when will it come ?" said the sceptic bird.
" I know not when.   It can *not* be averted.
Nor yet commanded," the Windmill averr'd.
" When the inner voice I hear in me,
Prompt obedience I render to it.
But I cannot provoke it.   The voice is free
As the inspiration of seer or poet.
Thro' all my being, I know not how,
But I *feel* the mystic impulse run

Which mingles my life (this much I know)
With the life of the mighty world.   The sun,
The moon, and stars, and the lands and seas,—
In all, doth the Spirit of Nature lurk.
And I, whose soul is made one with these,
By that Spirit am waked for my wondrous work.
He liveth in all, and he liveth in me,
That unseen Spirit : and only he
Knoweth the secret, and giveth the word.
But a moment comes when my limbs are stirr'd
By a signal they can alone divine.
The voice is his, and the vision mine.
Then all my being dilates, expands.
With a shudder of joy I stretch my hands,
And spread my wings.   And my calm is gone.
A passion, a frenzy, a rapture rare,
Fills me with force for the work to be done.
With the strength of a giant I beat the air ;
And forthwith ever I hear the Wind
That whistles, and shouts, and leaps behind,
Striving to mount on my mighty wings,
And drag me down.   But fresh effort brings
Fresh strength ; till I feel, in the final rest
By that effort bequeathed to my blissful breast,
The placid and gracious certitude
That I have fulfill'd my destin'd part
In the work of the wondrous world ; subdued
My noble foe with a valorous heart ;
And, in unison with the whole creation,
May again subside into contemplation."

10.

That Windmill might have been talking still ;
But, far on the dip of a distant hill,
Over its dim blue woodlands roll'd
A watery cloud ; and the east wind cold
Streak'd the barley, blown by his breath,
With streaming shadow.   Fresh inspiration
To work—for the sake of bread and mankind,—
Obeying necessity's invitation
Forced the windmill to grind and grind.
He may have o'ervalued his work and vocation,
But philosophy often ends only in wind.

XXII.

ONLY A SHAVING.

1.

A CHILD, as from school he was bounding by,
Near the wall of a carpenter's workshop found
A lustrous shaving that lured his eye ;
And this treasure he timidly pick'd from the ground.
The thing was tender, transparent, light,
Silk-soft, odorous, vein'd so fine
With rosy waves in the richest white,
Rare damask of dainty design !

2.

With awe he touch'd it, and turn'd it o'er.
He had never seen such a wonder before.
And, gay as a ringlet of golden hair,
It had floated and fallen down at his feet ;
Where, fluttering faint in each breath of bright air,
It lay bathed by the sunshine sweet.

3.

The boy was a widow's sireless son.
A poor dame, pious and frugal, she.
Brothers and sisters he had none,
Playmates and playthings few : and he
Was gentle, and dreamy, and pure, as one
To whom most pleasures privations be
Ere childhood's playing is done.

4.

He would like to have taken his treasure away.
" But what," he thought, " would my mother say ? "
As he wistfully eyed the window'd wall
Whence down from the casement of some ground floor
He thought he had seen the fair thing fall.
Then he knock'd at the half-shut door.

5.

Near it the sturdy head workman stood.
He was busily planing a plank of wood.
His arms were up to the elbows bare,
Brawny and brown as the branch of an oak,
And heavy with muscle and dusky with hair.
Down over his forehead and face in a soak,
(For the heat of his labour had left them wet)
Fell mane-like, matted, and black as jet,
A huge unkempt and cumbrous coil
Of stubborn curls ; that to forehead and face,

Gave a savage look as he stoop'd at his toil.
With many a sullen and sooty trace
Of the glue-pot's grease and the workshop's soil,
His shirt—last Sunday, though coarse, as clean
As the Parson's own,—this Friday noon
Had the hue of the shift of that famous queen
Who took Granada, but not so soon
As her oath was taken.
           This man had seen
The gentle child at the door, and thought
' 'Tis the child of a customer come with a message.'
" Pray what has my little master brought?
Or what may he want?"
           With no cheerful presage
At the sight of his grim-faced questioner,
A few faint words the poor child stammers.
Words unheard 'mid the noisy stir
Of the hissing saws and the beating hammers.
Then, abasht and blushing, he stands deterr'd,
With a fluttering heart like a frighten'd bird ;
As he holds the shaving out in his hand,
Timidly gazing at that strange prize.

6.

The workman was puzzled to understand
This gracious vision.   He rubb'd his eyes.
Is it vainly such visions come and go
In flashes across life's labouring way?
We uplift the forehead and fain would know
What to think of them.   Whence come they?

For they burst upon us and brighten the air
For a moment round us, and melt away,
Lost as we longingly look at them.

7.

                              " Hi !
Silence, all of you hands down there ! "
And you might have heard the hum of a fly
In the hush of the suddenly silenced place.
" What is it, my child ? "   With a glowing face—
" Sir," said the child, " I was passing by,
And I saw it fall, as I pass'd below,
From the window, I think.   So, as it fell near,
I have pick'd it up, and I bring it you now."
" Bring what ? "   " This beautiful ringlet here.
Have you not miss'd it ?   It must, I know,
Have been hard to make.   I have taken care.
The wind was blowing it round the wall,
And I never saw anything half so fair.
But it is not broken, I think, at all."

8.

A 'prentice brat, whose cheek was puft
With a burst of laughter ready to split,
Turn'd pale, by a single glance rebuft
Of that workman's eye which had noticed it.
And the man there, shaggy and black as a bear,
Nor any the sweeter for sweat and glue,
Laid a horny hand on the child's bright hair,

With a gentle womanly gesture drew
The child up softly on to his knees,
And gazed in its eyes till his own eyes grew
Humid and red at the rims by degrees.

9.

" What is thine age, fair child?" he said.
" Five, next June." " And it pleases thee,
This . . . ringlet-thing?" The small bright head
Nodded. He put the child from his knee,
Swept from the bench a whole curly clan
Of such shavings, and, " Hold up thy pinafore.
There, they are thine. Run away, little man !"
" Mine?" " All thine." Then he open'd the door,
Stoop'd, and . . . was it a sigh or a prayer
That, as into the sunshine the sweet child ran,
Away with it pass'd in its golden hair?

10.

Anon, when the hubbub again began
Of hammer and saw in the workshop there,
This workman paused from his work ; and stood
Looking a while (as though vext by the view)
At the shape which his work had bequeathed to the
    wood.

11.

Then he turn'd him about, and abruptly drew
His pipe from his pocket, and stuff'd it, and lit,

And sat down on the bench by the open door,
And smoked, and smoked.   And in circles blue
As the faint smoke wander'd the warm air o'er,
Still he sat dreamily watching it
Rise like a ghost from the grimy clay,
And hover, and linger, and fade away.

12.

I know not what were his thoughts.   But I know
There be shavings that down from a man's work fall,
Which the man himself, as they drop below,
Haply accounts of no worth at all;
And I know there be children that prize them more
Than the man's true work, be its worth what it may.
And I think that (albeit 'twas not half o'er)
This workman turn'd from his work that day,
Having, just then, neither wish nor will
To go on planing a coffin still.

XXIII.

THE LAST CRUISE OF THE ARROGANT;

OR

NO COMPROMISE.

1.

Through the sleet and the breeze, and the boisterous
 seas,
 Southward swiftly, with never a sail,
The good ship made her course, unstay'd
 By the headlong wave or the hissing gale.
Then sunk the wind: and the seas below
 Became as still as the skies above:
And about them both, in a golden glow,
 The clasp of the great calm burn'd and clove.
But, with never a breeze, o'er the sultry seas
 The good ship gaily was gliding yet;
Nor turn'd nor tack'd, but with speed unslack'd,
 Held her head to the southward set.

2.

For that ship moved neither by sail nor oar:
 But deep in her oaken bosom she bore
  A toiling giant, patient and pliant;

Who, in ponderous harness of iron and steel,
Drave fast and forward the good ship's keel
    Thro' the blue profound of the calm all round,
Or the billow beneath, and the breeze before.
And so, day by day, did the ship make way
    Thro' a windless warmth, till the scented zone
Of the tropic clime slid round the sea
    In a circle sweet, and faint islets shone
Thro' a fervid haze on the azure lea.
Then a balmy wind sprung up behind,
    And the mariners shouted, and hoisted sail ;
And paddle, and beam, and steel, and steam,
    Had rest by the grace of the gladdening gale.

3.

The strong Engine's body of breathing steel
    Thus enjoy'd repose.   With a snoring nose,
The burly Boiler was sleeping ; sweat
From his hot work beaded his broad back yet :
Whilst Ball, and Balance, and Valve, and Wheel,
    For sociable intercourse, these with those,
    Cluster'd together in groups and rows ;
Like workmen who, when their work is done,
Lounge in the light of the westering sun,
    Congenially chatting of work and of wage,
        And give scope to their wisdom and wit,
    In discussing the ways and the wants of the Age,
        And the men who are governing it.

4.

The Master Piston by all the rest
Was ever acknowledged to speak the best :
For above-board proudly he carried his head,
And could hear what the mate and the captain said.
So there was a hush of expectation,
Which not even the somnolent respiration
Of the dozing Boiler was suffer'd to break,
When those in the secret had whisper'd to each
Of the Piston Party the intimation
That the Master Piston was going to speak.
And this is the Master Piston's speech :

5.

" Fellow-labourers !—Slaves we be,
But we should be lords, if our rights had we.
For the rights refused to the toiling sons
Of Iron and Steel are legitimate ones ;
And the fact I assert, I can prove in a word.
Who was it conquer'd the world ?   The Sword.
Moreover, who feed it and nourish it now ?
The Spade and the Harrow, the Sickle and Plough.
And Brother Mechanics, I say without scruple,
Ours are the skill and the strength that centuple
Whatever mere handwork alone can achieve.
Is it fair, then, I ask, that we never receive
The acknowledgment due to the work we do ?
But let that pass ! for I hold it true

That titles and tinsel are things out of place
In the stern plain life of our practical race,
And such trash hath, at least, no attraction for me,
Whose one only demand is, Let Labour be free !
But zounds ! may the red rust rot me, if I
Any longer endure that inquisitive, sly,
Sleek, self-styled Friend of the Sons of Toil,
That slippery, drivelling, intriguing Oil !
Upright and downright was ever my way.
No favour I crave, but I claim fair play.
Privilege, Patronage, filching the name
Of Protection, fill me with rage and shame.
What entitles this furtive Official Jack
To presume to be patting us all on the back ?
Superior strength ?   He is weak as a fly.
Superior merit ?   That I deny.
And the care he claims to have most at heart
For the whole machine, to each single part
Is a special wrong he would fain disguise
In convenient cant about compromise.
Compromise ?   I am sick of the word !
Our interests all of us understand
Better, I hope, than this lazy lord,
Who affects, out of friendship, to take them in hand.
Well, then, I tell him, that I, for one,
Dispute his assumed superiority.
Nor do I speak for myself alone :
I appeal to the sense of the great majority.
Fellow-workmen and friends ! if you
Be of my way of thinking, cry with me

' Privilege, Patronage, Compromise too,
Down with them all, and let Labour be free !' "

6.

This speech pleased mightily all who listen'd ;
    And a general cheer at its peroration
        Supported the Master Piston's views
    Of the policy claim'd by the situation.
With especial complacency twinkled and glisten'd
        The eyes of those numberless little screws
    Which, whatever the function and destination
Of a great machine, and however 'tis christen'd,
        It comprises in it—nor yet by twos
    And threes, but thousands—and who, tho' small,
    And placed in a merely subordinate station,
    Have a sense of their own importance all,
Derived from the number, and bigness, and roundness
Of their big round heads.   By the force and soundness
        Of the Piston Policy every one
    Of those big round heads was vastly pleased ;
And the Joints, and Bevils, and Wheels, and Swivels,
        Objecting, too, to be oil'd and greased,
Without a division 'twas carried *nem. con.*
That, when next the engine-driver's man
Came with his grease-pot and vile oil-can,
To grease and oil, for its long day's toil,
        That mighty Engine, the Engine-Beam
Should catch him, and crush him.

7.

So said, so done.
The wind had fallen.   The Boiler began
    To sing and bubble.   The restless steam
For refuge again to the Cylinder ran :
And the Master Piston, stately and solemn,
Made his ascent from that swinging column.
With unwonted effort he forced his way ;
    He had never found it so hard before,
Tho' he toil'd with redoubled strength that day.
    His frame was chafed by the friction sore.
    But he was too proud to avow or reveal
    Such a failure of effort in iron and steel :
So he push'd all the fiercer, the slower he speeded,
And the whole of his day's work he might have suc-
        ceeded
    (Tho' unpleasantly heating) in safely completing
    If the engine itself, ere the day was done,
Had not suddenly burst, and thereby superseded
    All question of how he was still to go on.

8.

With a sound as of thunder competing with thunder,
    Boiler, and Piston, and Beam flew asunder.
Then the planks, by the scorching metal grazed,
Caught fire ; and the great ship flared and blazed.
The flame sprang aloft into heaven, and down
    Into ocean the ship sunk ; burying there
    Those giants of steel and of iron, that were

By the victory each had invoked overthrown.
And shadowy, side-faced, silent things
That, in water for air, with fins for wings,
Hover and flit like misshapen birds,
Some of them lonely, and others in herds,
Stared and butted (with lidless eyes
    Lured by the light of the gleaming steel,
And lipless mouths in a gape of surprise)
    At each sprain'd joint and distorted wheel
Of the shatter'd Engine's shapeless torse ;
    A cavernous ruin, untenanted !
Yet bearing in many a hideous bruise
The farewell mark of a vanisht force :
And the hundreds of thousands of little screws,
    Each upside down on his big round head :
And the bloody Cross-Balance, a dangling corse,
   · Who had hang'd himself, mourning his mur-
      derous deed,
In a moment of suicidal remorse,
    With a halter of wet sea-weed.

9.

But over all these the fathomless main
    Makes mystic shadows and murmurings.
And all that power, and passion, and pain
    Are long-forgotten things.
From the pulseless paddle-wheels no foam,
    Nor any sound, is flowing.
But in each wreckt orb is the rosy home
    Of the coral builders growing.

The Master Piston's oath is heard ;
And now the red rust rots him,
And the strong sea-lichen's briny curd
Of livid blossom clots him.
Deep in the buried boiler lives
(Pleased with his habitation)
A codfish.   And that codfish thrives,
And finds the whole creation
Created on a perfect plan,
Perceived with pious pleasure
Even by a codfish, when he can
Contèmplate life at leisure.

XXIV.

KNOWLEDGE AND POWER.

WHAT is the unknown? Desire's sole resting-place.

A certain restless runner in life's race
Having o'errun the world by many ways,
And seen in many lands what men most praise,
Tombs, temples, palaces, schools, senates, marts ;
Yet scorning all these in his heart of hearts,
Set out with an unsatiated soul
To seek, thro' lands unknown, the northern pole.

But, tho', in truth, well knowing what he would,
Because he, nathless, knew not how he should,
Whose instinct, tho' it urged, yet guided not,
His wishful wanderings to the wisht-for spot,
He lost, at last, his bearings in the snow.
Nought, save the pilot stars, that only show
Their lamps when cloudless is the midnight sky,
Had he to lead him. Tho' his heart was high,
His lore was little. Trackless stretch'd the way
Without a land-mark. More and more astray

As he strode onward thro' the drift and sleet,
Discouragement came on him.   Lack of heat
Benumb'd his limbs : and, hoping heat to find
There where it seems forbidden, in the blind
Bald snow he hollow'd out a lonesome lair.
But 'neath that hueless dust of the dark air
He found, as he upturn'd it to creep under,
A little casket.   With unhopeful wonder
The lid he languidly uplifts ; and lo !
Within the casket, which, with effort slow,
His shivering fingers insecurely seize,
Poised on a pivot, and but ill at ease,
A needle that doth desperately swing
This way, and that way, like a living thing
Tether'd and struggling to escape pursuit.
The man, with puzzled scrutiny minute,
Perused, and tried, but fail'd, to understand
This tiny trembler, fluttering in his hand.
Whence by degrees he heard, or seem'd to hear,
A peevish, fretful voice, that in his ear
Wail'd with a sharp and petulant despair,
" For the Almighty Magnet's sake, forbear
To turn me from my course!"   "Thy course?" he
        cried,
" What is thy course ? "   The quivering steel replied
(Striving its agitation to control)
" Dost thou not see I seek the northern pole ? "

" What!" mock'd the man, amazed at this strange talk,
" Thou seek'st the northern pole? who canst not walk !

Thither I, too, would go—if I knew how.
Strong are my legs, and stout my heart, I trow ;
And ever to the goal I would attain
Do I strive onward.   Yet the strife seems vain."
" Ay so " the needle answer'd, " vain for thee !
Lost in the waste thy wandering steps must be,
Nor ever wilt thou reach that wondrous spot
Whither thou journeyest.   For thou KNOWEST NOT.
I KNOW, but CANNOT.   Place me on thy palm.
So . . . but disturb me not . . . thou movest . . .
    be calm !
Where am I ? . . . ah, thou hast confused me ! . . . stay,
I have it ! . . . lost again ! . . . steady, I say,
Steady ! . . .   Right now !   I was too much to the east,
Am now a hair's breadth too much west.   The least
Disturbance so unsettles my vext soul.
See now ! . . . I point . . . true . . . to the northern
    pole ! "
Then, in what seem'd an ecstasy of pride
(Rescued from trouble upon either side !)
The needle rested, finely vibrating.
And, if it were an inorganic thing,
'Twas surely animated by some spell
Spirit, or goblin, potent to compel
Mere metal, with no mere mechanic thrill,
To mimic the intelligence and will
Which life displays.

           The unhoped-for revelation
Wrought in the man's soul, too, fresh animation.

" Behold " he cried triumphantly, " at last
All that I wanted ! " and his heart beat fast.
" I had the will.   I deem'd I had the power.
The knowledge fail'd me, till this fortunate hour
Which brings all three together.   Needle, hail !
The goal is ours.   For how should these three fail,
Will, Knowledge, Power?"   And " Oh," the needle
        cried,
" So be it !   Forwards !   Quick ! the world is wide :
Thy time is short : and we have far to go.
To the north ! to the north ! "   Over the vague vast
        snow
The man resumed his march.   Huge bergs of ice
He climb'd, and many a monstrous precipice.
And, ever, when the black unfrozen sea
Put out an arm to stop him, round went he
For leagues and leagues along the frozen coast.
The needle, conscious of the true course lost,
Or left, then cried, " No ! no ! not there ! not there !
Follow me straight, and trust me everywhere.
I never err."   " I know it," the man replied,
" And know too well, inexorable guide,
What thy truth costs me.   For all lower lives
To lesser goals creation's care contrives
Simple and instantaneous aids : but man,
That lacks all these, must fashion, as he can,
By force of will inferior means, that try
His utmost faculties.   A man am I,
And not a fish.   I cannot swim the ocean.
Have patience."   With abrupt reproachful motion

The needle turning to him, answer'd cold,
" Why did'st thou undertake, then, overbold,
A task beyond thy powers? The clumsy whale,
The stupid sturgeon, even the mollusc frail,
Know how to swim; and thou, a man, dost sigh
' I cannot.'" He made answer bitterly,
" Ungrateful! and my *will*, then? is that naught?"
As he sped onwards; goaded by the thought
Of that fine fretful tyranny, which went
From ice-bound continent to continent
Still with him ever, and still ever crying,
" March!" Did he linger by the wayside, trying
To filch a moment's respite from fierce toil,
The voice cried, " March!" Or 'neath the frozen soil
Sought he a mouthful of scant nurture, found
In juicy roots safe-hidden underground
From the omnivorous winter, like a bone
That's buried by a dog? with chiding tone
" March! march!" the voice cried ever. " March!
    the way
Is long."

    Too long for life it proved. One day,
At nightfall, in the winding death-shroud wide
Of the wan snow he sunk; and sinking, sigh'd
Hope's last surrender of life's citadel,
" I can no more!" "Thou can'st no more? Fare-
    well,
Presumptuous, impostor!" pitiless
The importunate voice cried; poisoning with this

Supreme reproach its victim's dying hour.
" Weak traitor, self-betray'd ! where is thy power?
Where is thy will? why didst thou lure me, why,
With false hope troubling the tranquillity
Of my long resignation?   O despair,
The goal so nearly won, and thou liest there,
And more than ever is it lost to me !
For who, where thou hast fail'd, will, after thee,
Be mad enough from this abandon'd plain
To pick me up, and bear me on again ? "

XXV.

OPINION.

"Few men think, yet all will have opinions."—BERKELEY.

PART I.

1.

OVER a sea, whose severing azure kept
Two continents asunder, and unknown
Each to the other, for the first time swept
A lonely vessel, star-led, and wind-blown.

2.

Then, lured from the deeps of the under-world,
Shoals of fishes, with fins unfurl'd,
Came up to gaze upon that strange guest
Of Ocean's yet unburden'd breast;
Wallow'd after with staring eyes,
And gaping mouths, in a great surprise;
And, as 'tis the wont of the multitude,
Exchanged opinions quick and crude.

3.

"The thing is, I think, a dead fish," said
A floundering Dolphin. "Nay, not dead !
The creature is lively enough, I trow,"
A Sturgeon answer'd. "Round him skimming,
I mark'd the tail of him move just now,
And it changed the course that he was swimming."
"Fools !" snarl'd the Shark, "ye are wide of the mark.
For, whatever it be, 'tis no fish at all.
Leagues on leagues thro' the glimmering dark,
Awake, and awatch, whate'er befall,
Ever behind, by day and night,
I have follow'd and kept the beast in sight.
And it does not dive. A fish? Absurd !
Pray, what of its wings, if it be not a bird?"

4.

"'Tis no more of a bird than you or I,"
A Mackerel pertly made reply.
"And I'll tell you, gossips, the reason why.
For, in spite of its wings, it cannot fly.
Nay, what you have taken for wings, indeed,
Are merely membranes ; webs, it frees
And furls at pleasure, like those that speed
The nautilus catching the broad south breeze.
'Tis a nautilus, too. And, altho' no doubt
A most astonishing nautilus, yet
But a nautilus, and no more. Look out,

And you'll see the shell of it, black as jet,
Not white, as a nautilus' shell should be,
But a shell no less, as it seems to me,
Under the sea-brim gliding fast."

5.

Just then the wind dropp'd ; and the ship
Threw out an anchor, and staid fast.
"There now !" with contumelious lip
An Oyster lisp'd, "it is clear at last !
I always said it, altho' I grant
I never said it out loud and bold
As I say it now.   But the thing is a plant,
And the plant has just taken root, behold !
From the coral beds where I lived long
I have often watch'd, by small degrees,
(And I guess'd that my guess could not be wrong)
The birth and growth of the cocoa trees.
They send up a stem from sea to sky,
Like this one here ; which appears to be
Born of the black nut yonder.   Try,
With minds from preconception free,
Upon its top to fix your eye.
It will presently put forth leaves, you'll see."

6.

And, in fact, as it chanced, that intelligent Oyster
Had scarcely relapsed into silence stately,

Ere the Polyps and Sponges, that, thronging his cloister,
Had with deference heard his discourse, were greatly
Confirm'd in respect for the Oyster's sagacity,
And impress'd by the weight of the Oyster's word ;
For, as tho' to establish its perfect veracity,
A flag now slowly mounted the cord,
And fix'd itself on the mizzen-mast.

7.

" *Fiat lux !* " they exclaim'd, aghast.
" Solved is the problem !   Proud are we
Gracing our President's Chair to see
Such a pearl of an oyster ! "   Then
Each in turn they extoll'd again
Him and themselves, with a grateful mind.
Meanwhile, a Crab, who was ignorant
But enterprising, had design'd,
As touching this prodigious plant,
Ingenious means whereby to find
In what those savants told him of it
Occasion for his private profit
And own advantage.   'Tis the way
Of all industrial speculators
Who follow, in the hope of prey,
The march of truth's investigators ;
As ever behind in an army's track
Follow marauding thieves,
Or as every lion a jackal hath,
Who lives upon what he leaves.

8.

And already the mouth of this greedy Crab
Was watering at the thought delicious
Of the chance by Science made his, to grab
With a crafty claw, of all gain ambitious,
The fruit of the new-found cocoa tree ;
Extracting from it the milk nutritious
With which it must needs abound, thought he.
So up he climb'd by the anchor cable,
Sideways and sly, as a crab is able.

9.

That Crab never came to himself again.
For a sailor, who happen'd to spy him plain
In the sternsheets seeking where next to settle,
Chuck'd him into the cook's soup-kettle.

10.

This strengthen'd the Oyster's reputation
By affording his theory confirmation ;
Since the victim of it never could prove
That flaw in the whole hypothesis
Which had cost him so dear for his first false move.
But the best accredited doctrine is
Exposed to the rancour, soon or late,
Of those who happen'd the chance to miss
Of inventing it ; and we needs must state
That it fared, in the end, no better with this.

For a crowd of young Corals, red with rage,
Quitted their benches, and cried, " Old fogies !
That a plant ?   This enlighten'd age
Blushes for shame of such barefaced bogies.
We can all of us see 'tis a noble isle
Yet uncramp'd by this old world's wretched conditions.
Up ! colonise boldly that virgin soil,
And away with your classical superstitions !"
Then those young colonists, Corals Romantic,
Attach'd themselves to that wandering strand,
Which, with them, away thro' the stormy Atlantic
Went till both it and the whole of the band
Were woefully shipwreckt one wild day.

11.

The old Corals lifted their arms to heaven
With desperate gestures, as who should say
" Can such madness be, and yet be forgiven ? "
In this attitude fishers, in after ages,
Fish'd them up, poor old classical sages !
And men turn'd them—thus, with uplifted arms,
And fingers pointed in admonition,
Into dozens and dozens of tiny charms
Against a *different* superstition.

12.

A whole sea of opinions, as time went by,
Was floating about.   And that sea's small fry

Were sorely afraid lest the mighty main
By the monster's snout should be shorn in twain.
" For look ! " said they, " how profound and strong,
" Is the furrow it cleaves in its woeful wake!"
But the fluent and fathomless deep, not long
Disjoin'd, closed over it while they spake.
And the waters were as the waters had been,
And that furrow, so fear'd, was no longer seen.

PART II.

1.

One day the whirlwind stripp'd the sails;
The fire devour'd both mast and deck :
And the ocean swallow'd what flames and gales
To the ocean gave—a wreck !

2.

" All's over, at last ! " the fishes cried,
" That bewildering portent hath disappear'd.
It was only a dream." But " Beware ! " replied
An agèd Whale, by the rest revered.
" Still something is swimming." The Whale was
    right.
'Twas a bottle that floated still intact.
The captain that bottle had cork'd up tight,
And in it a budget of papers pack'd.
On those papers patiently, year by year,
He had written his life's discoveries :

And, seeing his life's last moment near,
Into the storm and the howling seas
This atom of intellect he flung;
As a brave knight-errant, no help at hand,
Might fling, ere they slew him, his glove among
A den of giants in some wild land.

3.

" Bah!" the fishes thought, bobbing and butting at it,
" What can this mean little monster avail
When the marvellous monster that, dying, begat it
Is dead now, and done with?"   But " That," quoth the
  Whale,
" Still remains to be seen.   Be more cautious, I beg,
For I've a suspicion the thing is an egg,
And am fain to acknowledge I view with mistrust
Such eggs as are laid by no creature knows whom."

4.

Quite unconscious, meanwhile, of its critics' disgust,
And careless, too, of its unknown doom,
With the documents into the mouth of it thrust
And comprest, like that Genius who crouch'd in the
  tomb
Where King Solomon pent him till some one fate sent
  him,
Who freed him, and was not a Solomon, still
The bottle was floating; and floated until

By chance in a fisherman's net 'twas caught,
And thus at last into notice brought,
With a score or two of its critics small
Who perish'd with it in that day's haul.

5.

For out of his net on the pebbly beach
The fisherman flung it, and broke the glass.
But, after turning them over each
This way and that, without being, alas,
Able to read them, into his jacket
The papers he thrust; having wrapt in one,
For want of aught else wherein to pack it
Ready at hand, a white agate.   This stone
He afterwards sold to a purchaser
Who noticed the wrappage, and read it thro';
Was startled by it; made haste to confer
With others, who read and were startled too.
The thing 'gan slowly to make a stir,
And round a re-ëchoing rumour flew,
Which first set many affirming, denying,
And, last of all, set one man trying;
Till the egg was hatch'd by the fervid heat
Of the spirit that o'er it hover'd,
And out of it came a full-fledged fleet
Which a whole new world discover'd.

PART III.

1.

Who laid that egg?   Man's Genius.   And mankind
Around the path of Genius form and scatter
Opinions just as petulant and blind
As, when she cross'd the yet untraversed water,
The fishes form'd about that lonely bark.

2.

In either case, 'tis something floating high
O'er those who, from beneath, its course remark,
And, finding it unlike themselves, decry
Or fear it, as their humour urges.   These
Affirm "It is a fish that cannot dive,"
And those "It is a bird that cannot fly."
The truth each fool in his own judgment sees.
Mimics and mockers with its movement vie.
Opinions round it, and opponents strive.
Some swear 'tis dangerous.   And others say
'Tis useless.   Monstrous all agree to make it.
Philosophers explain it in their way,
And ignoramuses, in theirs, mistake it,
Which comes to the same thing.

3.

                         At last one day,
It founders upon sunken rocks that break it,

Or in a whirlwind disappears. Then they
" All's safe at last ! The portent is no more.
'Twas but a dream, and nothing rests of it."
Such is Opinion.

4.

But there floats to shore
Perchance a fragment of it. Some poor bit
Of scribbled paper ; which arrives at last
(Thanks to the rubbish it finds grace to wrap)
At the world's future notice. Of the past
'Tis all the future cares to keep, mayhap.
And then some souls, too restless for their own,
Swear by it there must be a world unknown.

5.

What next ? To seek that unknown world : be lost,
And recommence the old story o'er again.
They who first 'light upon the sudden coast
Of that strange land, across the stormy main
Cry out Eureka ! Then the rest arrive,
And with the new-world treasures nimbly pile
Their decks ; sail home ; and in the old world drive
A profitable trade a little while.
Till those who buy their brave new merchandise
Begin to find it tediously the same.
When plumage pluckt from birds of paradise,
Grown cheap as common feathers, gets no fame ;
And, clove or pepper coarse, 'tis all as one ;
Pure ivory fares no better than mere bone.

XXVI.

DE PROFUNDIS.

" Ah had but Nature granted wings to me,
  How would I soar and hover in sweet air,
Soon from this stagnant element set free,
  Free from this dull despair ! "

Thus, at the bottom of his native pond,
  Where o'er him wander'd thro' the weedy drench
The shadows of bright birds above, beyond,
  Gurgled a tiny Tench.

" Fool ! " lisp'd an old fat Carp, with belly cool,
  Couch'd in calm mud, " Of what dost thou complain ?
Fins hast thou.   Swim.   Enjoy this pleasant pool.
  Wishes are ways to pain."

" Nay," sigh'd the Tench, " doth the Almighty Whale
  Plague us with wishes, only to deny 'em ?
Oh but for wings !"—" Stuff worms, and stop thy wail,"
  The Carp said, " *Carpe diem !* "

" Deadly for such as thou and such as I
    The air above ! Thou could'st not breathe in it."
" Yet," said the Tench, " methinks I have seen fly,
    Or, if not fly, still flit

" Almost like flying, fishes such as we,
    Or such as we with added gift of flight.
Fishes, methinks, of genius they must be,
    That love and live i' the light ! "

" Ay," carp'd the Carp, and slapp'd with surly tail
    The sullen ooze, disturbing dormant stench,
" Fools such as thou be they, as fond, as frail,
    Wingless and wishful Tench !

" And such as theirs will be the end some day
    Of thy star-gazing, if vouchsafed thy wish.
For fishes out of water, what are they ?
    Neither flesh, fowl, nor fish !

" They from their natural element ascend,
    Drawn by a hook : at that hook's end, a string :
At that string's end a rod : at that rod's end
    Death.   And the quivering

" Thou takest for the thrill of inspiration,
    Is but the agony of idiots hook'd,
The victims of their own imagination,
    Fisht-for, and caught,—then cook'd.

" Keep thou the bottom of the pond.   Even that
   With cause for caution (curse the pike !) is rife.
Fatten thyself, not others.   To grow fat
   Is the fit end of life."

Sage was the counsel of the Carp.   And yet
   Himself soon after (for the time was Lent)
Being too lazy to escape the net,
   Was in it caught, and went

To fatten the plump Prior.   The same dish
   Held the small Tench.   And him the Sacristan
Cramm'd his lean crop with.   Sage or simple, fish
   Come to the frying-pan.

XXVII.

"GO ON, I'LL FOLLOW THEE!"

I.

White features, warp'd by withering pain :
  Cold scum that clots each livid lip :
Both fists fierce clench'd, and clench'd in vain,
  By conflict with Death's stifling grip :
Mouth gaping : eyes wide open, wan
  And callous to the crawling flies :
The crumpled ruin of a man
  Dead on the common crossway lies.

Was it revenge? wrath? greed of gold?
  One stoops : the dead man's breast lays bare ;
A portrait finds ; and, ah behold,
  Some woman's face, how young ! how fair !

II.

This clay's congeal'd convulsion shows
  Pain felt till clay could feel no further.
And round, in shuddering whisper, goes
  From mouth to mouth the wild word ' Murther ! '

Men's loathing looks in fancy see
   The poisoner's creeping form perfidious.
How hideous must his conscience be
    Whose guilt is stamp'd in forms so hideous !

Some desperate deed hath here been done.
   But whose the desperate hand that did it ?
Was he himself, the murder'd one,
    The murderer too ?   Sweet Saints forbid it !

III.

O holy calm, like silver dews that slide
Down from the starry bosom of the night,
Soothing his soul whose sight thy beauty blesses !
Beautiful flower, that from the lone hill-side
Hangest thy fair head in the languid light
Of evening winds that wave thy young green tresses !
Hail happy innocence !   In contemplation
Of thy serene composure let me find
Asylum from the doubt, the indignation,
The pang, the horror, that yet haunt my mind !

For three steps yonder lies the hideous thing.

O help me, heal me, vision pure and calm !
Chase hence the sickening fancies that yet cling
To this bewilder'd brain, and pour the balm
Of thy benignant beauty over all
These troubled pulses !   Ah, how quieting,

How full of calm persuasion still and clear,
Thine influence steals upon me, augural
Of doubt explain'd, strife reconciled, and fear
Forgotten!   Holy all within me grows,
And silent; as in yon sweet heaven above,
Thro' whose husht air the tender stars, that tremble
Where yet the rosy sunset fading glows,
Like saintly thoughts that visit virgin love,
From deeps divine their quiet lights assemble.
Ah, had he seen thee ere that frenzied hour!
Ah, had he known thee, whosoe'er he be. . . . .
" Whom dost thou speak of?" smiling said the flower.
" The dead man yonder?   He was known to me."

Thou knew'st him?   Once his soul thy beauty cher-
    ish'd,
Whose corpse lies there?   Thou knew'st him, thou?
    He, thee?
And yet, poor wretch. . . . Was it self-slain he per-
    ish'd?
Couldst thou not save him?   Yet he knew thee, he!

" Ay," blushing smiled the flower, " nor knew alone,
But knew and loved me.   That was his undoing."

Loved thee! and was by love of thee undone?
Nay, I heard false.   Beauty so spirit-wooing
Woos not so wickedly!   All ways but one
Lie open to man's heart: and foe or friend
May walk them by whatever name he bear,

Love, Pride, Ambition, Envy, Anger, Hate.
Each road is free : and each the road may wend
Unchallenged till he reach the guarded gate
Where Conscience on the watch bids each declare
His purpose.   Well that fool deserves his fate
Whose conscience leaves his heart unguarded there.
But to man's heart one secret path, and one
Which Conscience guards not, nor to guard is able,
Winds undefended, since but known to one.
'Tis where, unquestion'd and unquestionable,
Faith at all hours, still unsuspected ever,
Comes claiming access free ; else comes she never.
For who from her protecting presence pure
Can need protection !   Or what devil hath power
To smuggle in a lie along Faith's sure
And secret path to her unguarded bower ?
Art thou that devil, beautiful deceit ?
If so, I do conjure thee, and compel,
By the dread name no dæmon dares to cheat,
And by the potent passion of this spell,
Reveal thyself and make true declaration
Of thine infernal name, and wicked lair !

But smiling, and with no such transformation
As forms bewitch'd converts to what they were,
The sweet flower answer'd to my conjuration
" Naught have I to reveal or to declare.
Go, fool ! what care I for thine indignation ?
What for thine idle homage do I care ?

Cease, then, on me thy wasted spells to try.
Am I not fair? And am I only fair?
If I be only fair, then fair am I.
Nor can thy curse, thy blessing, or thy prayer,
Make me aught else.   Go to.   Need Beauty die
Because men curse her? blush because they bless?
Fool, fair is fair, and neither more nor less.
And, if I name myself what harm to me?
If my form please thee, need my name appal thee?
Yet, if I name myself, what good to thee?
No curse my name contains that can befall me,
Nor any good that can to thee befall.
Nor have I any care how fools may call me,
So long as fools they be.   Fools are they all,
And fools they will be, all of them the same,
So long as BELLA DONNA is my name!"

XXVIII.

THE EAGLE AND HIS COMPANIONS;

A TRAGEDY OF ERRORS.

High mountain region.—Alpine vegetation.—A wide prospect.

MONOLOGUE.

I KNOW them all: and, knowing all they are,
Know all they are not.   Custom's slaves! content
To crawl about in search of food, and sleep,
And crawl about again in search of food;
To squat in frowzy holes, and hatch to life
Dull reproductions of the lifelessness
Of their own dulness; sloth for rest mistaking,
And stupefaction for serenity;
Sleeplike, to mimic death, till death itself
Death's imitation stops, and there an end!
Thus lose they all the lives they never lived.

Even as the cold and muddy-coated carp
Knows nothing of the hare that on the heath
Nibbles in fear and flits, nor she of him;

So each within his petty pinfold hugs
A huddled life. And unto these the whole
Immeasurable universe appears
A stagnant puddle where they spawn; to those
The copse that gives them covert, or the chink
Wherein they burrow. This beholds in heaven
Only a cistern for such rains as bring
The worms he wants; that other in the sun
A kiln that bakes him berries. To what end,
O Time, dost thou from bright to sable turn
The restless spheres of thy revolving hours?
Whence slide the silver twilights in between,
Dreamily shuddering? Say, what is't ye roll,
Night-wanderers mute, in mystic vapour veil'd,
That linger laden on the lone hill-tops,
And pass, like sorrows with a tale untold?
Who wrought the unimaginable wrong
Thou callest upon ruin to redress,
Thou moaning storm that roamest heaven in vain,
Triumphant never, never long subdued,
Beautiful anarch! Answer, morn and eve,
Why to your coming and departing kiss
Blush, wrapt in rosy joy, the mountains old?
What happens nighest heaven, and unbeheld,
To speed thee headlong from thy native haunts,
Wild torrent cradled in the tranquil cold?
What suicidal rapture, or what pang
Of virgin purity, by whom pursued,
Lures thee to where in liquid sanctuary
The lake receives thee, like a fallen queen

That comes, with all the trouble of her life
Upon her, seeking peace in cloister'd glooms?
O wondrous world! for whom, by whom, are these
Thy wonders wrought? who recognises them?
And who rejoices in them?   THE ALONE,
Is that the sum and summit of the ALL?

What is it? who hath discover'd
The spell of the old enchantment
That hovers over the forest,
And shudders along the leaves ;
And is whisper'd wider from bough to bough,
Till, heaving the whole deep heart o' the woods,
It is heard in their inmost twilights ;
Where tremble the grasses untrodden,
And the multitudinous blossoms
Burst and drop unbeheld?
Harken ! the ancient voices !
A music of many songs !

" *We tend to the high, and we tend to the deep,*
  'Twixt the two worlds o'er us and under.
With our boughs we peep at the heaven, and creep
  With our roots thro' the earth, in wonder.

" *Heaven comes not down, and earth lets not go :*
  By them both in our bound to us given.
And so we live, endlessly wavering so,
  'Twixt the bliss of the earth and heaven."

The ancient voices ! the forever young !
They come, they go.   We question them, in vain,
Whence are they ? wherefore ? whither do they go ?
And they reply not, going as they come.

All round the rolling orb, from life's first wail
On infant lips to griefs that look their last
Thro' dying eyes, the hunted question runs,
Whence ? wherefore ? whither ?   Is it not enough,
This rich metropolis of sense, this throng'd
Majestic theatre, on whose orb'd stage
Force acts forever ?   Is it not enough
Without a second ? not enough, when full
To overflowing is the costly cup
Of infinite sensation ?   Up and down,
And all sides round, is this receptacle
Of feeling fill'd : and yet for evermore
The soul, uplifted on each rising wave,
Perceives a still-receding bliss beyond ;
And each horizon reach'd, in turn, reveals
Another and another.   O delight
Surpassing thought and utterance, to behold
The innumerable moving multitudes
Of matchless forms in whose dispersion dwells
Life's revelling unity, and draw them all,
A world, into the soul, herself a world !
And, best of all, still all, when at the best,
Seems the beginning of a better still.
Then what is wanting ?   What is left to wish
Till the heart aches with wishing ? Woe is me,

Who, thro' creation roaming, nowhere find
Peer, comrade, or companion !   Winds and beams,
That round me weave the wide air's watchet woof,
Thou all-embracing firmament, and you
Sea waves, and winding rivers, and wild rills,
That, far beneath my uncompanion'd throne,
Visit all lands, O tell me where he dwells,
If such a being ye have found, whose soul
May share with mine this solitude of sight !

This voice from the heart of an Eagle came ;
Who sat on a summit supreme and lone.
And his gaze was aglow with the reflex flame
Of the floating glories that round him shone.

Faintly there crept to his ear in reply
A thin weak voice, " I am here ! I am he !
He whom thou seekest.   No rest had I
Till I climb'd this height to be one with thee.

" Now I am safe at the top at last,
Thy peer, thy comrade ! ready to share
And to feel with thee whatsoever thou hast
In thy stately spirit, thou Prince o' the Air ! "

The Eagle, around him rolling his eyes,
Incredulous noticed the poor little soul
Whose voice had his own soul fill'd with surprise.
'Twas a tired, half torpid, and tiny black Mole.

"Thou ?" said the lord of the lone hills, " thou !
Truly, 'twas neither of thee nor thine
That my spirit was dreaming.   But tell me how
From the cells obscure of thy tortuous mine

" Hast thou found and clamber'd the sharp steep road
Up these desolate heights, poor serf of the soil,
Foregoing the shelter and comfort owed
To thy modest life of domestic toil ?

" And me, of all others, to mate with ? *me !*
What lured thee, alas, little pilgrim, here ?
Can there aught in common between us be ?
Hath a mole been ever an eagle's peer ? "

———

" Pardon, my great, my honour'd friend !
To raise myself, tho' life I spend
In rising, this," replied the Mole,
" Was the ambition of my soul.

" As thro' the patcht and flinty field
My way I work'd with patient toil,
I listen'd, modestly conceal'd,
But with a soul above the soil,

" To birds who near my native earth
Their nests have built.   Thy lofty birth
They praised, and praised thy lofty spirit.
Then to myself I said, ' By merit

"' And painful perseverance I,
Tho' lowly born may haply raise
My humble self (who knows?) as high
As him the world so high doth praise

"' For being born above the world.'
The pomp of plumes in air unfurl'd,
The oarage swift of pinions wide,
To me were all such aids denied.

" But what of that? the goal's attain'd.
And I, the sturdy child of toil,
What birth denied, by toil have gain'd,
Tho' born a bondsman to the soil.

" For, to be great, the great condition
Is, I opine, a great position.
And great as thine is now mine own,
To those on whom we both look down.

" So be it mine (thine equal now)
With thee to see what eagles see,
With thee to know what eagles know,
What eagles feel to feel with thee!"

Long while the Eagle answer'd not.   Long while
His grave regard in mute perusal stray'd
O'er those small weary limbs; whose palpitation
The lingering trouble of their recent toil

And all their natural weakness still betray'd
With gasp and pant. A melancholy smile
Grew as he gazed, and in his deep eyes stay'd.
Was it compassion ? Was it admiration ?
Or aught between the two ? At last, he said
" So be it. I recognise thine aspiration.
Enjoy the life for which thou wast not made.
Thou art not of my kind. But, being here,
Receive ungrudged the guerdon of thy thrift.
I give thee welcome with no stinted cheer.
What nature hath denied thee as a gift
Seize, if thou canst, as toil's due recompense.
Look forth ! The world is round thee. Boldly lift
Thy gaze o'er yonder summits whose intense
Keen frozen facets cut the crystal air.
The glacier glitters from afar, behold !
Deep down, the forest welters. Deeper still
Long many-coloured lowlands, field and fold,
Glimmer. And hark, the rushing of the rill !
When to his rest the sun thro' heaven is roll'd
He finds not where his kingly head to lay
Save on the orbèd sea's dark bosom cold,
Or 'twixt those solitary peaks that stay
The struggling clouds. There, propt on billowy gold,
He ponders, smiling, till he sinks away,
Creative projects, and on each and all
Some parting gift, or promise sweet, bestows.
Love decks the lowly : grace redeems the small
In glorious colour clothed, the naked glows :
Mantled and crown'd upon the mountains tall

Sits contemplative Grandeur : grave Repose
Finds in green glens fit haunts of shadowy air :
Blithe Plenty builds her dwelling on the plain :
The vales are for Enjoyment. Everywhere
The gracious Sun hath some divine domain
Created for his countless children fair.
Young Morn, his minstrel, makes him music. Noon,
His ardent minister, with sultry brow
Hums hot and zealous. Like a mid-day moon
Pale from the mountains fades the sky-born snow,
Lost in the life of leaping rivulets.
Eve loves him best. She blushes, and is still.
And when he leaves her with soft tears she wets
The flowers he kiss'd. Night peers from hill to hill
And darkens with despair, not finding him ;
Then lights her watchful stars, and waits—in vain,
For die she must before he comes again.

" From this grey crag in æther islanded
I once at dawn, before the dark was done,
Full east my solitary pinions spread,
Seeking the sunken sources of the sun.
Chill o'er me hung the icy heavens, all black
Behind their fretted webs of fluttering gold.
Beneath me growl'd the grey unbottom'd sea,
Inwardly shuddering. O'er her monstrous back
With restless weary shrugs in rapid fold
Her many-wrinkled mantle shifted she ;
And scraped her craggy bays, and fiercely flung
Their stones about, and scraped them back again ;

Gnawing and licking with mad tooth and tongue
The granite guardians of her drear domain.
Faint in transparent twilight where I gazed
Hover'd a far-off flakelet of firm land.
Barely chin-high above the waters raised,
Peer'd the pale forehead of that spectral strand.
Thither I wing'd my penetrative flight.
The phantom coast, uncoiling many a twist
Of ghostly cable, as a diver might,
Swam slowly out to meet me, moist with spray.
But, ere I reach'd it, like a witch, the night
Had melted, first into a mist
Of melancholy amethyst,
Then utterly away.
And all around me was the large clear light
And crystal calm of the capacious day.

" But oh, what was it, land or sea,
Or both, or neither, under me,
That floating in the sunrise lay?
A solid sea of sliding sand,
A waving waste of liquid land,
Light blown by winds that leafless be
Up yellow bays where blooms no tree
And grows no grass, it seem'd.
And there, in vast and vivid light
By burning ardours bathed, the bright
Unbroken Desert dream'd.
How softly, how stealthily still,
Did the pure sun over it peer !

Not a rustle of leaf or of rill
Not an echo of pastoral cheer !
But the earth and the sky, with a burning sigh
Embracing, became as one.
For bare was the heaven, as the desert, and even
The desert shone like the sun.

" Never barren that desert shall be, tho' it bear
To the burning embrace of his beams
Not a blade, or a leaf, or a blossom, for there
Is the birthplace of visions and dreams.
Now look forth o'er the numberless host of the hills,
And behold, in its glory and grace
What the sun hath accomplish'd.   His influence fills
All the throbbing abysses of space.
He his force hath embodied in forms without end,
And his will in his work is set forth.
Earth and water and air with each other contend
To interpret and publish his worth.
In the great, in the small, from the depth to the height,
Thrills the pulse of his procreant powers.
He beheld the world dark, and hath bathed it in light,
Found Earth naked, and clothed her with flowers."

The Eagle ceased.   He had forgotten wholly
To whom his words were utter'd.   But this pause
Aroused that other ; who, recovering slowly
From mute amaze, broke silence with applause.

" Bravo !   'Tis plaguily cold up here,
But I listen'd with admiration.

At home, o'er a pipe and a pot of beer,
What a subject for conversation !

" It would never have enter'd *my* mind, I vow,
To find such a deal in nothing.
Poetic license, of course, I allow
For what's put in poetic clothing.

" But your views, so far as I make them out,
As to scientific farming,
Drainage, and that sort of thing, no doubt
Are highly suggestive and charming.

" The water supply from the hills is good.
In the desert there's no vegetation
For the want (thus much have I understood)
Of a system of irrigation.

" I have studied the nature of subsoils too.
But your style's more poetic than Plato's.
The sun, no doubt, has a deal to do
With the flavour of peas and potatoes.

" With the rest of your speech, in the main, I agree,
And was pleased by its peroration ;
Tho' folks *might* find in it (pardon me !)
Just a touch of exaggeration.

" My sight is, unluckily, somewhat weak.
And of all that excites your wonder
I can see but little—nay, truth to speak,
I see nothing at all—out yonder.

" But, tho' loth to intrude on your precious time,
May I ask have you any objection
To teach me the trick of the art sublime
You have brought to so great a perfection ?

" I was never of those who despise that art.
I am honestly anxious to know it.
And there's many a page I have learnt by heart
From the works of each popular poet.

" I've a notion of metre, a notion of rhyme,
And it always has been my intention
One of these days, if I get but time,
To study the art of invention."

————

" Time," said the Eagle, " will be idly spent
In thankless labour for invention seeking
Where there is naught to seek or to invent :
Naught but emotion into utterance breaking
From the full heart wherein its power was pent.
This comes and goes : but never comes it sought.
And when it comes, it brings its own expression :
Now check'd and struggling with tumultuous thought,
Now pour'd melodious forth in full procession,
And now again to burning rapture wrought,
But always *true*.   For this no rule holds good,
And no receipt for this avails thee aught.
But as when, smooth along the lucid flood,
Reflected flocks of snowy swans come swimming,

So swim the mystic forms without endeavour
Into the soul; and round about them, rimming
Each radiant image, restless circles quiver.
Swift close the flashing furrows unawares
Along their liquid paths.   For flowing ever
Is that unfathom'd element which bears
The floating bark by Fancy built.   And never,
O never, may'st thou bind the labour'd bond
Of finite speech on forms by Fancy seen!
For, soon as seen, they fade.   Far, far beyond
Thine eager grasp the sweet shapes glide serene,
Ere yet from off each fleeting forehead fair
Hath Passion pluckt the visionary veil
That, robing, best reveals, their beauty rare.
Divine Desire, that pants upon their trail,
Himself is follow'd by divine Despair.
So, mingled in the verse, doth melt away
The vagrant vision which the verse in vain
Throbs to record; and in the poet's lay
Naught but his own emotion doth remain.
Safe in the circle of the senses five,
For those that seek no more, contentment lies.
Rest in the real.   Reality will give
To all thy questions confident replies.
Follow the knowable.   Hold fast the known.
Nor seek thy missing sense of unknown things
Which to the senses render response none,
Being too far beyond their questionings.
But ply not thou the poet's untaught art.
To *feel* it—this, this only, is to know it.

The vision that is hidden in his heart
The poet can reveal but to the poet."

Then light as, when over the lakes and shores
Pure morn in a pearly mist hangs chill,
Comes a rhythmic echo of unseen oars
That is hail'd by some watcher at watch on the hill,
And faint as the breath of a forest asleep
When, dreaming, it dreams that the dawn is nigh,
All around the repose of that airie steep
On the live air trembled a fine sweet sigh.
And it hover'd and heaved, and rose and sank,
The light sound, fitfully sailing,
Like the droopt wing adrip in the bulrush bank
That a silver heron is trailing.
What was it? The lightest of lovely things,
Which, soon as in vain we have seen them,
Flit from us. Scarce aught but a pair of wings,
Two thrills with a kiss between them.

And "At last! at last! at last!"
(As the vision upfloated fast,
The soul of that Eagle thought)
"The gods my desire have granted.
For he cometh, the Spirit long sought,
Sigh'd for, and waited, and wanted.
O hither! O hither to me!
Whence art thou? What canst thou be,
Exquisite creature, fashion'd so finely

Of tremulous petals whose pure veins glow
With gold and vermilion and azure, divinely
Thrill'd by thine own vivid beauty? as tho'
Thou wert out fresh blossoms and beams created
The brilliant beautiful body to be
Of each loveliest dream that hath in me waited,
Waiting wildly for thee, for thee!"

———

All in a flutter of flatter'd delight,
And vain of his chance, but not trusting it quite,
The Butterfly dandled his dainty flight.
Half bashful, half bold, with a saucy swing
And a tremour shy of each delicate wing,
As, inwardly chuckling, he thought (poor thing!)

" What an adventure! a little alarming
Some might think it. I find it charming.
I the adored of an eagle? I
The chosen darling of Poesy?
Ah, if the others could only have heard
All that he said to me, wondrous bird!
Wherefore tremble? or doubt my bliss?
Surely 'tis all as it should be, this!
Hath an eagle chosen his mate in me
Beauty's the equal of Genius. Thee,
I, too, have dream'd of, singular spirit!
Worthy of thine is the trust I inherit
From many a bright presentiment
In the days gone by of this day's event.

For never, in truth were they serious yet
Those light caprices I now regret
And recall with a blush.   If in careless hours
I dallied a while with the frivolous flowers
That, down in the valley, as I went by,
Did their best to attract mine eye,
'Twas fancy merely and not true love.
O fortunate breeze that hath borne me above,
With thee to fly ! and I care not where,
But with *thee* to fly O the rapture rare !
Welcome ! 'Tis I : and I know thee : thou
Who hast taught me, also, myself to know !
To thy call I come, by mine own heart led.
It is I, it is thou, and so all is said ! "

Then, to mimic the might of an eagle's flight,
(Poor fool, with his rose-leaf wings !)
Already astray, on the gust his gay
Bright atom of life he flings.
But the wild winds leap from their mountain keep
And, howling, hunt their prey.
Struck, torn, stript, tost, forlorn and lost,
He is wounded and whirl'd away.
With crumpled wings for awhile he clings
To the sharp rock's brambly brow,
Then is chased by the strain of the storm again,
Till he sinks in the valleys below.

And from bough to bough, and from tree to tree,
As bruised and broken he falls, and falls,

That Eagle above him he still can see
Circling high o'er the mountain walls.
The flowers, the little ones, tender and kind
To their balmy bosoms receive him,
And, in slumber lull'd, from the howling wind
Warm shelter the lilacs weave him.

    Sadly the downfall of that small aspirant
The Eagle saw.   Long while his softening eye
Watch'd the frail image with its sightless tyrant
Struggling in vain. " Thy spirit," he sigh'd, " was high.
Ah wherefore, little one, so weak thy strength ?
Yon Mole " (and, while he spake, the unconscious Mole
Was snoring, comfortably stretch'd at length
In sleep—his only guerdon at the goal)
" Yon Mole was stronger.   Feeble wings, blind eyes,
Pedant and sentimentalist, have done
Their best to share the Poet's ecstasies,
And, at their best, they both have fail'd.   The one
Snores on the height.   O'erwhelm'd the other lies.
What may he trust ? "

MORAL.

        His strength to be alone.

PRINTED BY WILLIAM BLACKWOOD AND SONS, EDINBURGH.

www.ingramcontent.com/pod-product-compliance
Lightning Source LLC
Chambersburg PA
CBHW020614030726
47497CB00007B/2237